CRIME

INTERRUPTED

A BUCK TAYLOR NOVEL

BY

CHUCK

MORGAN

Printed in the United States of America

First printing 2017

ISBN 978-0-9988730-1-5

LIBRARY OF CONGRESS CONTROL NUMBER
2017918394

DEDICATION

3

This book is dedicated to my friend Sandi.

An incredible woman who has accomplished some amazing things in her life and is destined to accomplish many more.

Live your life to the fullest.

Chapter One

     Buck Taylor climbed over the
parapet and in a crouch run, made his way
to the front wall and knelt next to La
Plata County Narcotics Office Terry
Rubin. It was 5 AM on a hot July morning
but the night air still had that little
bit of coolness that comes from being in
the mountains at 6,500 feet. Terry had
located a great surveillance location on
the roof of Guy's Auto Body Shop on
Girard Street directly across the street
from Colorado Overland Transportation.

     Colorado Overland Transportation
was a small trucking and distribution
company located in Durango, Colorado and
for the last couple days had been the
subject of a huge surveillance net that
had been dropped over it thanks to Buck
and a host of local and federal law
enforcement agencies. This had not been
an easy task, coordinating all these
varied elements in a relatively small
mountain community without raising the
suspicions of the locals. So far Buck
was confident they had pulled it off.

Buck Taylor was 6 foot-tall and weighed in at 185 lbs. Very little of it flab for a 58-year-old man. Buck's hair was salt and pepper, with what seemed like a lot more salt than pepper and he wore it slightly longer than was typically the fashion of the day. Buck was always pleased when he looked in the mirror, since other than getting older, he was in as good a shape as he had been when he played defensive linebacker for the Gunnison High School Cowboys, back what seemed like a long time ago. He still tried to jog 5 miles every day when he could, and he tried to ride his mountain bike every weekend, weather permitting. The bike was always hanging off the back of his state provided Jeep Grand Cherokee. Except for a couple sore knees, coming mostly from age, Buck was in good shape, which was important in his line of work.

Buck Taylor was an Investigative Agent for the Colorado Bureau of Investigation. He was currently assigned to the CBI field office in Grand Junction, Colorado, but he hadn't really been in the office much during the past year. Somehow, he had become the favorite "go to" guy for the Governor of Colorado, Richard J Kennedy, who was in fact one of "those" Kennedys. The Governor had been in office about a year and half and Buck had been instrumental in closing several high-profile investigations during that period, that made the Governor look good and as a result, when a situation came up that might get a little hairy, the Governor always asked to have Buck assigned.

And that was how Buck ended up on a garage rooftop at 5 AM on a hot July morning. A week ago, Buck was in Teller County, working with the Teller County Sheriff's Office on a multiple victim homicide. The case had stalled while they waited for the State Crime Lab in Pueblo to complete some DNA testing and with a little bit of down time, the first he had had in a while, Buck had been standing hip deep in the South Platte River in Eleven Mile Canyon playing a real nice 16" German Brown Trout when his phone signaled that it was time to stop.

Chapter Two

Fly fishing was one of the hobbies Buck had used during the past year to help him get through the loss of his wife of 35 years. If you ask Buck, he will tell you that he fell in love with Lucinda Torres the first day of their senior year in high school. Lucy, on the other hand, would always tell people that Buck stalked her all senior year before she finally gave in, mostly to shut her friends up, and agreed to go to the movies with him. She had always considered him just another jock, another football player who was too full of himself. What she found on that first date was a shy, unassuming gentleman, for lack of a better word, who it seemed, cared more about pleasing her than in bragging about his prowess on the football field. She would tell people it was love at first sight that had taken a year to accomplish. From that day forward, they were inseparable.

During senior year Buck had been approached by several college football scouts who wanted to sign him to play for their schools. Gunnison High School was a pretty small school back in 1978 and Buck and his family were amazed at how many schools had noticed him, but for Buck college just wasn't in the cards. Buck hated school and spent a lot of time getting himself out of trouble instead of getting an education. When he found something that interested him, he had no problem learning all he could about the subject, but regular school work just bored him. After several long heartfelt discussions, first with Lucinda and then with his parents, he had decided to join the Army after graduation. Surprisingly, no one was surprised.

Buck had spent four years after high school in the army and by the time his enlistment was up he had been promoted to First Sergeant. He had spent three years of his enlistment in the Military Police and had really taken to police work. That was when he decided to apply for a position with the Gunnison County Sheriff's Department. Since he was already well known in the county he had no trouble getting a position as a patrolman. He proposed to Lucy on the night he received the call that he had gotten the position. His career was now set, and his life was set, and he made the most of his time with the Gunnison County Sheriff's Office, eventually becoming the Under Sheriff in Charge of the Investigations Division and coming to the attention of the Colorado Bureau of Investigations.

Buck had worked with the CBI on several investigations inside the county and had earned the respect of the investigators he had worked with. As twilight started to fall on Buck's career and knowing that unless he wanted to go into politics and run for Sheriff, that he had reached the highest position in the Sheriff's office that he could obtain. He really loved his job, but when the offer came in from the CBI, he sat down with Lucy and had a long heart to heart talk. He had spent 17 years in the Sheriff's Office and always figured he would retire from that job. They had three children, two in high school and one not too far behind and he was a well-respected member of the community. Did he really have the right to disrupt all their lives and pick up and move to someplace else and start all over? The kids had friends, Lucy owned a small deli/ice cream parlor and they had a good life. He could stick it out for another 10 years and retire and they could travel and see the world like they had always planned. Twice he turned down the offer from CBI, although more and more he felt like he was trapped behind a desk instead of doing what he loved, which was investigating crime.

The final offer came directly from Tom Cole, the then Director of the CBI. Buck always remembered the day. The

Denver Broncos had just lost another game, the third one in a row and his friends had all packed up and headed home when there was a knock at the front door. Now, anyone who lives in a small community knows that no one ever used the front door, and no one ever knocks. Who could this possibly be this late on a Sunday evening?

Buck answered the door and was taken aback to see the Director of the Colorado Bureau of Investigations standing on his front porch. The Director smiled and said, "Before you close the door in my face, please listen to my offer."

Buck invited him in and he and Lucy sat on the couch and listened as the Director laid out his plan. He was opening a new Branch office in Grand Junction that would house five agents and a small forensics unit. Buck could continue to live in Gunnison but would have to report into the office in Grand Junction twice a month, otherwise he would be free to work out of his house. No disruption in his life other than having to spend some time on the road as his investigations warranted. He would mostly work alone, but he would have the resources of all the branch offices at his disposal.

Before Buck could say a word, Lucinda said, "Buck, this is what you have been waiting for, a chance to be a real investigator again. You have to take this." That was one of the things that made him love Lucy every day. She always knew what he was thinking and she always understood what drove him. She had nailed it this time. Buck looked at the Director and replied, "Well I guess it's settled, looks like you have a new investigator on your team."

That was seventeen years ago and essentially what led Buck to be on this rooftop at 5 AM on a hot July morning.

Chapter Three

The sky was Colorado blue without a cloud in it and the fish had been biting furiously all morning long when Buck hooked in the big Brown Trout. After a good fight he felt the trout finally give in and he scooped it up in the net. What a beauty it was. The spots on the side of its body glowed in the noon day sun and Buck just held it in the net and admired it for a minute.

Buck loved fly fishing. He was a firm believer in the old adage that time spent fly fishing was not deducted from your life clock. In the year since Lucy's death he often wished he could have gotten her interested in fly fishing. He would have liked to have the extra time with her. He also relished the fact that when you are standing hip deep in the middle of a river you had to concentrate on fly fishing. Fly fishing isn't complicated, but it is complex, and it takes all your focus. When you are casting a tiny bug imitation to a big rising trout, you must be focused. And once focused, everything else just clears out of your mind. For a minute it is just you and the trout. All the other day to day stuff goes away.

He had just pulled his phone out of his wader pocket to take a picture when the phone lit up with an incoming call. It was his day off and he almost didn't answer it, but that was never a good career move when the Director of the Colorado Bureau of Investigations was calling. Buck hit the answer button.

"Hope I didn't get you in the middle of something important." Said the Director, Kevin Jackson, before Buck could even say hello.

"No sir, just doing a little fishing until we get the DNA back from the lab."

"Good" the Director replied.   "I hate to interrupt a man while he's fishing, but this is important."

Buck listened carefully as the Director explained the situation. Since Buck was on hold in Teller County the Director wanted him to head down to Durango to meet with the La Plata County Sheriff. It seems the Sheriff and her team had come across a possible drug distribution network working out of a small Durango based shipping company and it could have possible Mexican Cartel links. The Sheriff was worried that this could morph into something big and she wasn't sure she had the budget or the manpower to run a full investigation. She was requesting help from the CBI. He could use his own judgment on whom to involve if the information checked out, but he wanted it played low key until that decision was made. No sense getting the locals all fired up about drug cartels moving into their small town until all the facts were in.

Buck hung up the phone, removed the trout from the net and held it in the water facing upstream to revive it and watched as it streaked back towards the pool he had pulled it from. The sight of trout streaking through the water never failed to mesmerize Buck. He gave a silent prayer of thanks to the "river gods" for allowing him the privilege to catch the fish he caught today and headed for his Jeep. He hung his wet waders on a hanger he had fashioned so they could dry while hanging in the car and he broke down his four-piece 5 weight Orvis Clearwater fly rod and placed it back in its case. Finally finished stowing his gear, he took one last look at the river, got in his car and headed back down the dirt road he had followed in a couple hours ago. It had been a good day. Time to go to work.

Chapter Four

Durango, Colorado, population about 18,500 sits along the Animas River in southwest Colorado, not too far from the border with New Mexico. It is the county seat of La Plata County and the jumping off point for the Durango and Silverton Narrow Gauge Railroad. A dramatic train ride from the city of Durango to the City of Silverton, topping out at over 12,000 feet in elevation. Mostly a quiet mountain town until Fort Lewis College is in session and then the local police have their hands full with underage drinking and minor drug issues.

An outdoorsmen's paradise where hunting and fishing abound and the home of the Purgatory ski area. Lately more and more people called it the Durango Mountain Resort. I guess they don't like the idea of skiing in Purgatory although the locals still call it Purgatory, mostly out of a sense of history and probably to piss off the new comers who changed the name. By all accounts a perfect place to raise a family and live

the good mountain life. Durango has all
the amenities of a larger city in a self-
contained small package. The kind of
place where everyone knew everyone else
and knew a lot about each other's
business. Not the kind of place that a
Mexican Drug Cartel would try to use as a
base of operations.

First thing the following morning
Buck met with the local Sheriff,
Elizabeth Sinclair, and her Narcotics
Officer, Terry Rubin. Liz, as she
preferred to be called, was a seasoned
twenty-year veteran of the Sheriff's
Department who decided to run for the
office when long time Sheriff Ed Maxwell
decided to retire and go fishing in
Florida. Liz had easily won the election
since she ran unopposed and was now in
her second term at the helm. She was
smart, dedicated, the mother of two and
grandmother of four and had been married
to Ross for almost 30 years.

Buck had met Liz on several
occasions and was extremely impressed
with her knowledge and experience. He
had never met Terry Rubin before and was
surprised when the young man, probably in
his early twenties, walked into the room.
Of course, being Buck's age made pretty
much everyone younger than him, but this
young fella looked like he had just
graduated from high school. He stood 5'9
and weighed about 150 lbs. soaking wet.
He had a bald head and a small scruff of
what you might call a beard on his chin.

The most striking thing were the tattoos that completely covered both arms.

Buck grabbed a cup of coffee from the counter in the meeting room and introduced himself to Terry. After a little small talk, they all sat down at the conference table and settled in for a review of what they had so far.

"Buck" the Sheriff started. "Thanks for getting down here so quickly. I only spoke with Director Jackson yesterday morning."

"No problem, Liz. Happy to help."

The Sheriff smiled. "Terry, why don't you take Buck through what we have so far."

Terry pulled a pair of reading glasses from his pocket and opened the file he had in front of him.

"The information we received came to us last Wednesday from a local drug dealer and meth head I busted." Terry went on to explain that Carlos Montoya, AKA "Scratch" because he was constantly scratching at his arms until he was nothing but scabs, had been busted trying to sell thirty Oxycodone pills to a local high schooler and had been dumb enough to do it right in front of the kid's parents, who immediately called the Sheriff's Office. The family lived just outside the city limits which is how the Sheriff's Office got the call. Since Terry had had dealings with "Scratch" before, he knew exactly where to find him and arrested him in Fanto Park with the help of a Durango Police Department patrolman.

Buck held up his hand. "How screwed up is this guy and can you believe anything he has to say?"

Terry thought for a minute and replied, "In all the time he has been around, and this is not the first time he has tipped us to something going down, he has never lied to us."

"Keep going officer."

Terry now dug into his notes. "Right after we brought him in he told me he had something big to tell me if we could keep him from going up to the state penitentiary in Florence. He wanted to stay in Durango to serve whatever time he got. I told him I would see what I could do, but the info had to be good. Really good."

Terry went on the explain that "Scratch" had told him that he had gotten the drugs from a local company fronting for the Sonoma Cartel and that he had seen huge crates full of drugs in a warehouse right here in Durango and that they were planning to start shipping these drugs all over the western and southwestern US in the next week. He didn't know exactly when but soon. What also came out was that he wasn't supposed to have the drugs, but he had put a bunch of pills in his pocket for safe keeping while he watched the Mexican prisoners break the pills into small packages and hide them in kids toys.

Buck started to say something, but the Sheriff cut him off. "We are not sure what the Mexican prisoners is all about, but we think they may have a small labor force of illegals that they keep in the back of the warehouse, almost like prisoners. One of the clerks at the grocery store says that one of the employees of the shipping company came in the other day and bought a huge amount of food and water."

Chapter Five

Buck nodded, and Terry continued the briefing. Terry had set up a surveillance nest at his Brother in Law's auto body shop which was right across the street from the trucking company and with the help of two other deputies had been watching the company for the past couple nights. They noted several trucks coming in at very early hours in the morning and unloading several large crates. Colorado Overland Transportation was a small shipping company that had a decent amount of business, mostly local and regional shipping until last week. This week there are nine semi-trailers in the yard and about a dozen people loading the trailers. Seems like business had suddenly boomed for the small trucking company.

Everything up until night before last looked like typical trucking business and we had no way to see what was in the crates. That all changed. At about four AM one of the laborers or prisoners, whatever you prefer, tried to make a break for the fence, which is always kept locked. As the deputy on surveillance watched, it looked like he threw something over the fence before he was tackled by two big goons and beat senseless. The two goons hauled him back inside and they closed the freight doors and locked the place down.

The deputy, hoping not to blow the surveillance, waited for about an hour and then left his post to see if he could find what was thrown over the fence. At this point Terry slid a box across the table to Buck. What Buck was looking at was what looked like a brand-new action figure in a sealed box. He opened the box, pulled out the figure and looked at it carefully.

"Pull off the head." Said Terry.

Buck grabbed the head and with a slight twist pulled it off. He then turned the figure upside down and a pill fell out from inside. First just one, but the more he shook the figure the more pills fell out until he had a pile of about twenty pills lying on the table in front of him. To say he was surprised would be an understatement. Buck had seen a lot of weird things during his many years in law enforcement, but this was a new one.

The Sheriff got a very serious look on her face and said "Now you see why we called you guys. This could be huge. What do you think?"

Buck thought for a minute before answering. His mind had moved into what he called investigation mode and he was already running several scenarios around in his head. He took a long sip of his now cold coffee. "This could be a big problem." He looked at Terry. "Officer, you have done some good work here. We need to nail down the shipping schedule and I need to make a couple phone calls. Let's meet again at three o'clock. Is there an office I can use?"

Terry excused himself and Buck and the Sheriff walked back to an empty office just outside the bullpen. The Sheriff looked concerned. She had seen Buck move into Investigation mode and when it happened things moved quickly.

"How big a problem do you think we have?" She asked. Although she already knew this was serious.

"I think we have a big problem. If this is the Sonoma Cartel, then they have moved into the US a lot faster than anyone anticipated and that won't be good for anyone. We are going to have to move a bunch of people into town and keep this whole thing quiet as we can while we do it. Please keep the team that you have on this on a short leash until we get this worked out and let's keep observing the warehouse. We need to know if anything changes that might indicate the time line is speeding up."

With that Buck walked into his temporary office and closed the door.

23

Chapter Six

Colorado Overland Transportation was a small company that suddenly had a great deal of business. The small trucking company was started 5 years ago by longtime friends Hector Vegas and Richard Dillon. This was their third attempt a starting a business together and the only one that seems to have grown legs and was still in operation. Hector's mom had died a few years back and had left him a small inheritance, about $45000, and after talking with his buddy Dick, they decided to buy a truck and become truck drivers.

Surprisingly, even to them, they found a little under developed niche and concentrated on delivering goods to shops and businesses that operated along the Colorado New Mexico border. Now a lot of this area was part of the Southern Ute reservation and as it turned out a lot of companies didn't like doing business in "Indian Land." That never bothered Hector and Dick. They had grown up in this area and knew how to make things

work so that the money kept coming in.
Within a couple years they had grown to
four trucks and four drivers and had for
the most part gotten off the road and
into the office of the new warehouse they
had leased.

Both men were married, Hector to
his 3rd wife, and they each had a couple
kids. They each bought a nice middle-
class house in Durango before the real
estate boom hit and prices went through
the roof. All in all, they looked like
two guys who had finally found their
little piece of the American dream. They
had bank accounts, belonged to the PTO
and the Elks Club and had even helped
start the Downtown Business Association,
which was great for them since the little
mom and pop businesses in downtown
Durango were their bread and butter.
Every year at the holidays they
contributed to the downtown holiday
lighting display and their wives helped
set up the annual Winter Festival. All
outward appearances said these guys were
fine upstanding members of the community.
In the last ten years, they hadn't even
gotten as much as a parking ticket.

There was nothing in their
backgrounds that would have led anyone in
law enforcement to look twice at these
guys. At least that is what they had
both been hoping for when the lure of big
money came walking in their door one day
a month back in the guise of Ernesto
Salvatore. Ernesto pulled into the yard

in a brand-new Mercedes AMC turbo, which immediately got the attention of their Office Manager Claire Ringsby. Ernesto walked into their office, confident as you please, and asked to speak to the owner. Claire, sensing something good, ran into the back and pulled Hector off the phone. Hector was the only owner in the office. Dick had gone to Mancos to deal with a problem client and wouldn't be back for a while.

Hector walked up front and extended his hand," Hector Vegas, I'm one of the owners, how can I help you today?"

"Ernesto Salvatore, Attorney at Law. I represent a client who is looking to give a lot of business to a local trucking company and after doing a little research, believes you might fit the bill. Is there someplace we can talk privately?"

Hector led Ernesto back to his private office and closed the door after telling Claire he was not to be disturbed. Hector had seen "Slicks" before and he sized up Ernesto. Expensive shoes, expensive suit and a briefcase that probably cost as much as Hector's car. Definitely a "Slick", Hector thought to himself. But if his client could afford this mouth piece then maybe they could be in for some big money. Hector decided to listen to what the lawyer had to say.

Hector sat down on the edge of his desk and pointed to the chair. Ernesto put his briefcase on the desk and sat in the visitor's chair and looked at Hector.

"Mr. Vegas." Began the lawyer. "I am not here to blow smoke up your ass. My client is willing to invest heavily in your business and towards your continued success provided you are smart enough to see a great opportunity when it pops up in front of you. Once a month my client will be bringing in shipments of toys and other goods from Mexico and Central America. They will arrive by truck, be off loaded into your warehouse, redistributed in additional trucks that we will provide you with and the drivers to drive them. We will supply all the laborers to do the redistribution and cover all the costs for their upkeep and for this we will pay you and your partner one hundred thousand dollars a month each. All you need to do is make sure that this happens on schedule and that this whole operation is kept as quiet as possible."

Ernesto sat back in the chair and looked at Hector. Hector had heard a lot of stories in his day but this one was over the top. This guy just offered him and Dick one hundred grand each to basically do nothing except store some stuff and watch a schedule. What was the catch? And so he asked.

Ernesto didn't seem taken aback at all with the question. He explained that his client was a wealthy importer who was interested in expanding his import business into the Southwestern US and needed a discreet business partner to make this possible. He told him that his client had many competitors who would love to see him fail, thus the secrecy. Ernesto removed a laptop from his briefcase and open the cover turning it so that it was facing Hector. The screen was blank. He then looked directly into Hector's eyes.

"One thing you should know. This decision has already been made for you. You cannot reject this offer, all you can do is accept and follow the rules."

He pushed the enter button on the laptop and on the screen was his wife and youngest daughter in the kitchen of his house baking cookies. The picture was from inside his house. How could that be? Ernesto pushed the enter key again and the screen now switched to someplace in the desert. The screen showed a man kneeling on the ground with his hands tied behind his back. As Hector watched in horror another man walked up behind the kneeling man and with one swipe of a machete chopped off his head. Hector could not believe his eyes. Was this for real? It couldn't be, could it?

Ernesto closed the laptop and sat quietly, letting what Hector had just seen sink in. After a minute, Ernesto spoke. "That man was a Federal Police Officer assigned to a small town just south of the border. He had agreed to work for us and then had a sudden change of heart. We took care of the problem and that changed heart is no longer beating. Now we are not saying that the same thing could happen to you or your partner or your beautiful families. All you need to do is accept our money every month, keep your mouth shut and act like nothing is happening. If you can do that we will get along just fine."

With that Ernesto put away his laptop, removed two bank account receipts for a bank in the Cayman Islands, each showing a deposit of one hundred thousand dollars and put his business card on the desk, closed his briefcase and stood up. Hector just sat there stunned. His mouth still hanging partly open, unable to speak.

"Tomorrow a construction crew will arrive to build some dormitory rooms in the back of the warehouse. In the next couple days, you will receive nine more slightly used semis and nine forty-foot trailers, all properly licensed, insured and registered. You will continue to operate as normal. Nothing changes. Someone will be in touch with you in a week or so with the first schedule. Do this right and you will be rich men and have access to all your wildest dreams. Mention this to anyone or damn up the schedule and you will live to regret your life. Have a nice day, Mr. Vegas."

With that Ernesto opened the door and walked out of the office, said a fond farewell to Claire, got in his car and drove away. Claire walked back to find Hector siting at his desk looking dazed.

"Hector are you alright?" She asked sounding very concerned.

Hector looked at her and told her he was fine and that he didn't want to be disturbed until Dick got back. Claire left his office not certain what, if anything, had just happened.

Chapter Seven

Buck sat back in the chair in his temporary office. He had his fingertips together making a small steeple out of his hands and he had his eyes closed. Buck was not sleeping. What he was doing was organizing the investigation in his head. They had a lot of work to do in a minimal amount of time and he wasn't going to have a lot of time for organization once he started. The yellow pad on his desk sat empty.

Going to war against a local street gang was hard enough but going to war against a cartel, especially the Sonoma Cartel, was incredibly dangerous and Buck was going to be putting a lot of people in the crosshairs. This whole operation had to be done in secret and his entire team would have to have their identities protected. Cartels had notoriously long memories and even longer reach. No one will be safe.

Every federal law enforcement and intelligence agency had issued notices about the Sonoma Cartel during the past year. According to what Buck knew the

Sonoma Cartel was a relatively young organization that had suddenly burst on the scene about two years ago. It was run by a major psychopath named Carlos Rojas. Rojas had been a minor player in the Los Angeles drug world when he was arrested and deported back to Mexico. He found a home with several of the cartels as his reputation for brutality grew. He became almost a legend. There was no one Rojas wouldn't kill for a price and it was said that sometimes he didn't need a price to kill. His signature was headless, limbless torsos, left on doorsteps, for all the world to see and to send a message that disloyalty would not be tolerated.

It wasn't long before Rojas got tired of working for someone else and he started turning on his overlords. He recruited a huge crew of psychopaths with the same penchant for violence he had and started taking out the leadership of the various cartels he had freelanced for, taking over territory and amassing a huge fortune in a very short time. It was estimated that he was personally worth over a hundred million dollars and his cartel had a bigger budget than a lot of third world countries.

The more Rojas moved forward, the more bodies piled up. He didn't care if you were a cop, a judge or a mom with three kids. If you crossed him, you were dead. It was a very simple plan. The Mexican government was powerless to stop him. The US government also feared that Rojas had his hand so far into the Mexican government that they would never be able to stop him.

Buck put his hands down and picked up his phone. Director Jackson answered on the second ring.

"How bad is it?" The Director asked.

"I think it's about as bad as it could get. The Sonoma Cartel has possibly moved into Durango."

There was silence on the other end of the phone. Buck just waited. "Are you absolutely certain? Up til now there has been no sign of them moving into the US. This will change the game significantly if you are right. Damn!! Do you have a plan?"

"I am working on that, but the problem is the timeline is real short."

Buck went on to give the Director as much of a briefing as he had been able to put together, explaining the need for secrecy, and laying out the bare basics of a plan. There were a lot of moving parts and when he was done the Director said, "Alright. It doesn't sound like we have enough evidence to get a search warrant, so we will need to put some assets in place who can get that. Do you think the Sheriff has enough to get a local judge to issue a wiretap warrant?"

"I think we can get that. Once we show the judge what we have, it should be enough to scare the shit out of him. That's usually a pretty good motivator."

"Ok", said the Director. "Start that ball rolling. I need to speak to the Attorney General and the Governor."

"Right. I was also going to call my local contacts at DEA, FBI and ICE. We are going to need all the help we can get." We are meeting again this afternoon at 3. I will send you a number so you can ring in. Later."

Chapter Eight

Buck hung up from the Director and speed dialed Hank Clancy. Hank was the Special Agent in Charge of the FBI's Denver Office. Buck had worked with Hank on several occasions and they seemed to hit it off. Hank was a hardnosed, by the book agent and Buck knew if he could convince Hank of what they had, he would have no trouble with the others he needed involved.

Hank answered his phone on the second ring. "I always hate it when your name pops up on my caller ID. It's never good. How the hell are you Buck?"

Doesn't anyone say hello any more.

"If you hate it, then this is really going to make your day." Buck proceeded to tell Hank the overview of the situation. Like the Director, Hank didn't interrupt until Buck took a breath.

"Damn Buck" He seemed to be hearing those two words together a lot today.

"This is our worst fear come true. Washington is going to go nuts. Are you certain of the connection'?

"As best we can. We have an iffy witness, surveillance video of a lot of activity in a tiny company and a doll full of drugs thrown over the fence by an illegal who we can't talk to because they probably either killed him already or beat him up pretty good. We will try to get a warrant to go electronic, but we are really on a short time line here."

"Alright. Here is what we need to do." Said Hank. "I need to call Washington and fill them in. I will talk to the US Attorney General and see if we can use a FISA warrant so we maintain secrecy all around. Talk to the rest of your local network and I will talk to you in a while. Do you have anything planned for strategizing yet?"

A FISA warrant is a secret document issued by the United States Foreign Intelligence Surveillance Court, which was authorized in 1978 by an act of Congress. Its primary function is to issue FISA Warrants authorizing secret electronic surveillance of suspected foreign spies operating inside the US borders. Due to increases in terrorism, the secret court had also, of late, been issuing warrants to surveil any bad actor, foreign or domestic, who posed an imminent threat to the people of the

United States. The Sonoma Cartel certainly qualified.

"Yeah." Three o'clock in the Sheriff's conference room."

"Good." Replied Hank. "I will try to get back to you before that. Damn. I really do hate when you call." Hank clicked off.

Buck wrote down the next name on his yellow pad and dialed the next number. Jessica Gonzales, DEA Agent in Charge of the Grand Junction field office, answered her phone.

"Buck Taylor. How the hell are you brother? It's been a long time."

"Hey Jess. Good to hear your voice. You doing anything right now? I have a little problem and could use your help."

Jess replied. "I'm not going to like this am I Buck?"

"No Jess. You're going to really hate it."

Once again Buck went through his briefing and once again he got the same response.

"Damn Buck, this is huge. We have been looking at these guys for months and thought they were contained in Mexico. This is gonna cause a shit storm."

Buck liked Jess. She didn't hold back on how she felt, and she had the

mouth of a truck driver. When the shit
hit the fan there was no better person to
have covering your ass. She was a tough
as they come and incredibly resourceful.
And unlike a lot of her counterparts, she
had no problem working with the locals.
Sometimes it seemed like she almost
enjoyed it.

Jess said. "Let me talk to some of
my people and see if we can get some
corroboration from the field. I can't
believe they could get this set up this
fast without there being some kind of
chatter about it."

The conversation Buck had with
Robert Townsend the local ICE Agent in
Charge went pretty much the same way, but
of course Townsend's questions were more
indicative of his position as lead
enforcer of immigration laws.

"Buck, any idea how they were able
to sneak a bunch of people into Durango
without drawing attention to themselves?
Seems like we may have a hole in our
system."

"Right now, Bob, we are too early
into this to know anything for certain.
Hopefully, once we get a little deeper we
can find the hole and plug it up."

"Okay. Let me get some people into
play and I will get back to you in a
couple hours. Thanks for reading me in
on this Buck, much appreciated."

Buck sat back and checked his watch. Already past lunch time and he had about an hour and half until he needed to meet with the Sheriff again. Time to grab a bite to eat.

Chapter Nine

Buck left the Sheriff's Department, hopped in his car, turned left out of the parking lot, turned left on US 550 and headed north. At 7th Street he turned right until he got to Main Avenue, turned left and pulled into the first parking space he found. Just down the street was his lunch destination. The La Bon Cafe.

Buck didn't speak a lick of French but he knew one thing, the La Bon Cafe was neither La Bon whatever that meant or a cafe. What it was, was a 20-foot-wide hole in the wall, sitting between a local book store and a real estate office. Mostly it was a bar with about fifteen stools and six small tables along one wall. It was dark, musty and usually smelled like stale beer, amongst other fine cooking aromas. However, what it lost in atmosphere it made up for by having the best burgers in Durango.

Jimmy Palumbo looked up from where he was wiping the bar down after the lunch rush and blinked twice when he heard the front door open.

"Son of a gun, that looks just like Buck Taylor, in the flesh. But I must be dreaming cause he ain't been around in a couple years to visit his old pal Jimmy." Nobody says hello any more.

"Jimmy is that you or is that your older, fatter brother? How the hell are you and how's it hanging?" Buck responded.

"Same as always." Jimmy replied, "About a foot long give or take." Jimmy laughed, he loved that line and he bellowed every time he used it, which thankfully wasn't often. Then Jimmy walked around the bar and gave Buck the biggest bear hug he'd had in years, or probably since the last time he saw Jimmy.

Jimmy Palumbo, now here was a real character. Jimmy was a bear of a man. Six feet six and two hundred seventy pounds and a good bit of it still muscle. He had grey hair tied up in a small ponytail and a neatly trimmed grey beard. He was dressed as always, jeans, T-shirt, that usually had a rude saying on it, but you usually couldn't read it because of the full apron he wore. Jimmy, with his girlfriend Loraine, were the proprietors, bartenders and as he liked to say, "head chefs of this fine establishment."

Jimmy was a transplant from Detroit by way of Southern California. At least that was the story most people heard. Although no one ever got the true story, it was told, mostly as legend, that Jimmy once rode with the Hell's Angels in Southern California and had to bug out when things got a little hot with the law. And he definitely looked the part. He had tattoos on every piece of visible skin and he had a very light scar on the side of his face, which was only visible when he shaved off his beard which hardly ever happened. However, Jimmy's appearance and his blood-stained apron made for quite a picture.

There was a soft side to Jimmy as well, which mostly only the locals got to see. Each year around the holidays, Jimmy would open his place and serve free food to the homeless and less fortunate. A charity event never happened in town that Jimmy wasn't a part of. And if anyone suffered an illness or a disaster, Jimmy was the first one in line to lend a hand, whatever it took. Deep under all that outside bravado was a simple man with a heart of gold.

Buck grabbed a seat at the bar and Jimmy threw a huge burger patty on the grill. Jimmy never asked you your order. If you were sitting at the bar or a table, you were there for a burger. That's all Jimmy sold. He didn't have chicken or salads and he definitely didn't have anything gluten free or

vegan. Jimmy was all meat and French
fries. Sometimes this surprised the
tourists but the locals all knew the
program and at lunchtime the bar was
usually packed, and Jimmy would be
standing behind the bar at the open
grill, sweating, regaling folks with tall
tales and cooking up a storm. Loraine,
his longtime girlfriend, usually was at
the register, taking in cash and handing
out to go orders. They were quite a
team.

Jimmy set a tall glass of Coke in
front of Buck then turned back to the
grill.

"Where's Loraine?" Buck asked.

Jimmy responded without turning
from the grill. "Her momma had a heart
attack about two weeks back and Loraine
went back to Detroit for a while to take
care of her, since her brother is a
worthless piece of shit. She's supposed
to be back a week from Sunday." Jimmy
flipped Buck's burger and sprinkled it
with a little salt and pepper.

Jimmy looked over his shoulder and
said. "We were sure sorry to hear about
your wife. Ya doin OK?"

Buck's eyes got a little misty.
Funny how a year had passed and that
still happened sometimes when he thought
of their time together. "Yeah, mostly
good. Still hard to believe she's been
gone almost a year now."

"Loraine was all broken up when we
heard. She always liked Lucy. We kept
waiting to hear about a service, but no
one knew anything. You keep it private?"

"It was supposed to be. Lucy
didn't want a service. She wasn't much
about religion and it was just like her
to want to keep things low key. She
never liked being the center of
attention. We had agreed that I would
scatter her ashes in the Gunnison River.
There was a little spot with a
handicapped fishing dock and she used to
love to have me wheel her down there and
we would just sit for hours and she would
watch the birds. She really loved that
spot."

Buck started to choke up a little.
He took a sip of his Coke and composed
his thoughts.

Jimmy said. "Hey, it's OK Buck,
you don't need to relive it. Sorry man."

"No. It's OK. It gets easier each
time I talk about it."

"I made plans with the kids to
scatter the ashes early one Sunday
morning. It was just supposed to be
family. I should have known something
was up. The park was never that busy on
a Sunday morning. We all gathered on the
dock, the kids and the grandkids and
Lucy's brother and his family and her
mom. Her dad had passed a couple years
before and her other sister was out of

the country. We all said a few words, and everyone got to sprinkle some of the ashes. When we finished and turned to head for the cars, we were stunned. There must have been three hundred people standing quietly behind us. I don't know how they all gathered so quietly. I guess word had gotten out that we were going to be there and everyone who knew her showed up. It was amazing. People had brought food and it turned into a huge picnic. Lucy would have loved it."

Jimmy handed Buck a handful of napkins and Buck wiped the tears from his face.

"Thanks for sharing, man. I can see that was hard." Jimmy turned back to the grill and used the bar towel to wipe the tears from his eyes. It was quite a sight.

Chapter Ten

Turning from the grill, Jimmy walked over to where Buck was sitting and leaned in. "You on the job?" He said, almost in a whisper. Buck and Jimmy went back a long way and sometimes Jimmy had some useful information to share and Buck knew he could trust Jimmy to keep quiet.

Buck leaned in a little closer so that the four other customers still in the bar couldn't hear.

"Yeah. Working on something with the county. What have you heard about a large distribution network being set up in Durango?"

Jimmy turned back to the grill. "You want cheddar cheese?" Buck nodded yes. Jimmy came back to the table and set the plate down in front of Buck. The burger was a huge half-pound of some of the best beef Buck had ever tasted, topped with lettuce and tomato and a mile-high pile of golden-brown fries. It looked like it could feed a family of four. Buck dug in not realizing how hungry he had actually been.

Jimmy walked over to the register and checked out two of his last four customers and refilled the beer glasses for the other two and came back round the bar.

"Can't confirm anything, but Dick Dillon was in here a couple weeks ago, really pissed and drinking pretty hard. Kept putting his head in his hands and crying. Couple times he asked God to make sure his family didn't get killed and how if he ever got out of this he was going to kick the shit out of Hector and that he didn't want any part of it. Finally had to call his wife to come get him before he fell down and hurt himself."

"His wife say anything?" Buck asked.

"Just that him and Hector had a fight about a new business partner and Dick was scared. She didn't know why and I didn't want to push her. Was gonna mention it to the Chief next time I saw him but then this thing with Loraine's mom hit and I pretty much forgot about it. You think this might have something to do with what you are working?"

Buck knew that whatever he said to Jimmy would stay right here. Buck had first met Jimmy fifteen years ago during a homicide investigation. Buck was still

new with CBI and he was working with his
mentor, Phil Mitchell, a grizzled,
seasoned veteran of forty years of police
work and one of the best investigators
Buck had ever worked with. One night him
and Phil accompanied two Denver Homicide
Detectives to interview a known drug
dealer about his possible involvement in
a recent murder. This was only going to
be an interview and it should have been
simple, but it went south in a big hurry.
The guy they went to interview was
waiting for the cops with a couple of his
friends and had no plans to go back to
prison.

As soon as they walked into the
location and announced themselves, all
hell broke loose. The two Denver
narcotics detectives were both hit and
seriously wounded, Buck dove for cover
behind a desk but Phil wasn't that lucky.
The first round went in just under his
armpit, where his ballistic vest didn't
cover. The second round hit him in the
neck. The coroner would later say that
either round would have killed him
instantly. Buck was pinned down and
returning fire when this mountain of a
man who looked like one bad ass biker
came charging in firing his weapon as he
was going. At one point a bullet raked
across his cheek leaving a deep bloody
gash but he kept shooting.

By the time the cavalry arrived,
the four bad guys were dead. Buck had
been hit twice in the chest, but the vest

had protected him. It still hurt like hell.   The big guy who saved him hadn't been wearing a vest. He was lying against another desk, with blood dripping down the side of his face and three gunshot wounds in his chest and right arm. Buck had been putting pressure on his chest wound when the ambulance arrived. Every day since, he thought about how Jimmy Palumbo's heartbeat kept getting weaker and weaker the harder he pressed to slow the flow of blood.

Jimmy was a ten-year veteran of the Denver Police Department and had been working undercover with the drug gang for the past two years. He wasn't even supposed to be at the location that night but had forgotten a gift for Loraine that he had left in the office. He had gone back for it and had just walked in the back door when he heard the detectives announce themselves at the front door and shooting started. He had no choice but to get involved.

Jimmy was in recovery for ten days and in rehab for ten months before he was told he could go back to work. The doctors said that if it wasn't for Buck, Jimmy would have probably bled out. Jimmy never forgot that. By the time rehab was over Loraine had convinced Jimmy that maybe a change of scenery was in order. Reluctantly Jimmy agreed but he never once looked back. Jimmy and Loraine ended up in Durango, after bouncing around Colorado for a few years, fell in love with the town and bought a small closed restaurant and bar.

Buck checked his watch and got off the stool. Even though Jimmy would never charge him a dime for the burger, Buck left a twenty on the bar. "Put that in the charity jar, OK?"

Jimmy nodded, and Buck headed out the door.

Chapter Eleven

Buck entered the front door of the Sheriff's Department and was buzzed through the security door, by the Deputy on duty. He walked back to his temporary office to gather his notes and headed for the conference room. He expected that for now it would only be the Sheriff and Terry Rubin. He was surprised when he walked in and found his boss, Director Jackson, Hank Clancy, FBI and Jessica Gonzales, DEA sitting at the table. Before he could say anything, the Sheriff and Deputy Rubin walked in and closed the door.

Hank Clancy looked like a typical FBI agent and Buck liked to tease him that his underwear was probably government issue. Today he wore his typical FBI uniform. Dark suit, white shirt, striped tie and shiny black shoes. Hank hadn't always been a bureaucrat. In his long tenure with the bureau he had been involved in some of its most high-profile cases.

Jessica Gonzales was one tough girl. Raised in Brooklyn, New York, she was the youngest DEA agent, male or female, ever, to be offered a position as an Agent in Charge. Buck had no idea how old she was and was afraid to ask. She had a thirteen-year-old son from a previous relationship and they lived with her mother. Jess was about five feet four, weighed about a buck twenty-five and was all muscle. She prided herself on her less than one percent body fat and worked out most days for two or three hours. She was also proficient in several different martial arts styles.

Today, her grey hair was short and spiked. She wore jeans, laced up boots and a black T-shirt that accentuated some impressive curves. It was rumored that she had several tattoos, but no one Buck knew had ever seen them. Her record at DEA was impeccable.

Kevin Jackson, the Director of the Colorado Bureau of Investigation was the youngest of the group. He had a stellar career with the Colorado Springs Police Department before being tapped for the top post at CBI. He was more bureaucrat than cop, having spent most of his career on the administrative side of things, but he was well respected in law enforcement and so far, Buck was impressed with him.

"I guess we all know each other so let's get started." Said the Sheriff.

As Buck took his seat he said. "I'm surprised to see you guys here. What's going on?"

Hank Clancy was the first to respond. "We spoke with the Attorney General, the US Attorney for Colorado and the District Attorney for La Plata County. Pretty much burning up the phone lines from here to Washington. Everyone agrees this is bad news. The problem is we need more definitive proof that the Sonora Cartel is involved before we can really move. So, after talking with your Director, my Director and Jess's Director, and since this is still a local investigation, we are here strictly in an advisory capacity."

Buck looked confused and started to comment but was shut down by his boss.

"We are all on board with this for right now. Everyone understands the urgency but right now it's not federal. It is still a local matter. Now, in order for this to move forward, we are going to bend a few rules. I will let Hank continue."

Hank opened the folder that was sitting in front of him. He slipped a copy of a document across the table to the Sheriff and to Buck. Just then the conference room door opened and a Christine Brewer, the La Plata County District Attorney walked in and sat down in the empty chair next to Buck. Christine had been the District Attorney for the past twenty-two years and at sixty-four years old she was looking to retire in a year or two. She had graying blond hair and hazel eyes and carried probably twenty pounds more than she wanted on her five-foot six frame. Buck had seen her in action in the courtroom during several of the cases he had worked in the area over the years and she was a formidable woman. She nodded to Buck as she sat down and removed a pair of reading glasses from her jacket pocket.

Hank spoke up. "First, we invited Christine here because for the moment, she will be responsible for getting any warrants we need. Now for the good stuff. The document in front of you is a copy of the FISA warrant, I just received by secure fax, which will allow us to set up electronic surveillance on the location. Now since we are only here to advise, I need the lawyers in the room to cover their ears for a minute."

Christine Brewer laughed and made a feeble effort to cover her ears. Everyone at the table laughed.

Hank continued. "I have a "sneak and peek" team on the way down from Denver. They should be here by nine tonight. They will get as much eavesdropping equipment into the warehouse as they can. They are aware of the guards, but a lot of what they can do will happen right from here. They will tap phones, computers and basically anything they can find by doing various sweeps. They will also try to get a camera into the space. This team is very good. They will set up here at the Justice Center and monitor everything they get set up. If we can confirm electronically that the Sonoma Cartel is involved, directly, then the investigation will switch over to us. Buck, you will still be lead agency. We will move from an advisory role to an assistance role."

Buck looked up from the warrant and looked at his boss. "This all makes sense, but I want it to be clear that this has been Deputy Rubin's case from the start and it will continue to be no matter what turn this thing takes. CBI is here by invitation from the Sheriff. She is the overall authority having jurisdiction on this. Clear?"

Everyone at the table nodded in agreement and Buck could see a small smile cross Terry Rubin's face.

"Now, so we can keep track of everyone. Your team will report to Terry here, and Terry will coordinate a couple Deputies to act as overwatch from across the street. We do not know how the bad guys are armed or even how many of them there really are, but I want some of our guys to back up your sneak team in case something happens."

No one made any objections, so Buck continued.

"Tomorrow morning Terry and I will re-interview his informant, "Scratch." I want to put my own eyes and ears on this guy. Terry can you get him over from the jail by eight AM?"

"Can do." Terry replied.

It was then that Buck looked at Jessica Gonzales. "Jess, what is the DEA bringing to the table?"

Chapter Twelve

Jess passed around a couple printed documents. "What you have in front of you is everything we have on some of the operators we believe might be behind setting up this distribution network. It's not much. We did find out that there has been a little chatter along the border about a big thing coming soon. Our guys failed to pick up on the importance and my boss is seriously pissed. Because of that I have been ordered to put my resources, and any other resources we might need, at your disposal."

"Basically, my job is to save the DEA's collective ass. Because we have an unknown time line I have also dispatched a DEA SWAT team. They will be staying at a hotel in Farmington, so as not to arouse suspicion and will be posing as a group of fishermen. One of our guys in New Mexico is a real-life river guide, so this works perfectly. We are also continuing to shake the bushes to see what we can find out."

Hank chimed in. "The FBI SWAT team will arrive tomorrow afternoon and will be staying at a small resort up near Wolf Creek pass. Their cover is a small conference for a startup tech company. Their vehicle is being driven down as we speak and will be parked behind the Sheriff's office."

Buck smiled. "This sounds a little more like assisting than just advising." Sly smiles all around the table.

For the next hour or so, the group discussed rules of engagement, safety and what direction the investigation would head in. It was also agreed that the "sneak and peak" team would GPS tag all the trailers in the yard just in case they started to move as separate loads instead of as a group. There were still a lot of unknowns and this bothered everyone in the room.

Buck finally stood up and checked his watch. "OK except for Terry and his guys, let's call it a day and we will pick this up tomorrow morning at ten. That will give us time to maybe get some electronics in and talk to our snitch. Thanks everyone for your advice."

Everyone got up from the table and small conversations started throughout the room. Director Jackson approach Buck who was talking with Jess and the Sheriff. "Buck, a minute."

Buck led his boss down the hall to his temporary office and closed the door. Buck took the seat behind the desk and the Director one of the two chairs in front.

"This is going to get a whole lot bigger before we are done. Do you need me to send down some help?"

"No sir. As you can see, in the next couple days I am going to have all the help I need. Hopefully it will be enough. These are good people."

"That they are." Agreed the Director. "I am heading back to Denver tonight. Keep me posted and if you need help, yell. I will send down the Cavalry."

The Director stood up, shook Buck's hand and walked out the door. Buck sat back for a minute and just shut down. A lot had happened since he had arrived in town little over eight hours ago. He hoped it would be enough. He had glanced at the info packet Jess had put together. If any of these were the guys involved, they were some scary dudes. Buck stood up, turned off the light and walked out the door. Tomorrow was going to be a long day.

Chapter Thirteen

"Are you out of your damn mind!"!

Hector had never seen Dick this pissed off. Dick turned around and slammed Hector's door. It made the whole building shake.

"You let a supposed cartel guy just walk in here and take over everything we have done here. Have you lost your damn mind?"

"Dick, he never gave me a chance, there was no discussion, I swear I wouldn't have done it, but he had a live feed of my wife and daughter from MY house. What the hell was I supposed to do?"

"You should have grabbed this guy by his neck and thrown his ass out the door. That's what I would have done."

"Dick...keep your voice down. They may have tapped our office like they did our houses."

"Don't tell me to keep my voice down. If you assholes are listening, then hear this. Go the fuck to hell. We ain't doing this, so shove your money up your ass. There now let's see how they react. God damn, Hector."

"Dick come on, man. We are talking about our families here. They cut off a guy's head while I watched. Scared me shitless'.

"Probably some Hollywood bullshit special effects and you fell for it. What a damn idiot."

"Come on Dick, this is serious. You weren't here. You didn't talk to this guy. We have to do this."

Dick turned the door knob and swung open the door, which banged hard as it hit the filing cabinet behind the door. Dick walked out.

"Where ya going? Come on Dick. We need figure this out. Dick come on."

Hector sat down in his chair. His whole body was shaking. He was scared of the cartel guys, but he might have just lost his best friend and put his family in jeopardy. Claire Ringsby stood in the doorway.

"You guys OK?" She asked.

"Not even close. I did something really stupid, but I had no choice." He put his head in his hands. "I had no choice."

Claire looked at Hector sobbing and didn't know what to do. She closed the door and walked back to her desk. Dick was behind her desk on the radio dispatching one of their regular drivers to pick up an order in Ignacio and bring it back to the warehouse. It was bound for Salt Lake City. No matter what that idiot Hector had done, Dick still had a business to run and he wasn't going down without a fight. He put down the radio, smiled a stupid little smile at Claire and told her to close up the office and take the rest of the day off. Then he walked out the front door, got in his truck and left. Claire knew exactly where he was going. Dick was heading straight for the nearest bar. She had no idea what was going on, but she was very concerned.

Dick parked outside the LaBon Cafe and tried to control the shaking in his hands. He really needed a drink but once he started he wasn't sure he'd be able to stop. He had promised his wife that he would cut back on his drinking, but this was something different and he had no idea what to do. He shut off the engine, climbed out and headed inside.

There were only a couple locals sitting at the bar, so he headed for a stool down the end, away from everyone. Said hey to the guys as he walked by, grabbed a seat and said hey to Jimmy. Dick ordered a beer and a double shot of tequila. Downed the tequila and ordered another. Took a sip of beer and just stared at the wall. Jimmy had seen people like this before and wisely decided not to ask if he was OK. It would either pass with a few drinks or he would eventually fall down. The drunker Dick got, the louder he got. Jimmy and the other fellas in the bar just let him rant. Dick was a shitty drunk and everyone knew it. Eventually Jimmy started watering down his drinks and stopped taking his money off the bar. Jimmy called Dick's wife to come get him. The last thing he said before he passed out and fell asleep at the bar was,

"That damn Hector. If they don't kill him I might."

The guys at the bar helped load Dick into the front seat of his wife's car and then went back inside to finish their drinks. Jimmy had heard enough of what Dick was saying to get the feeling that something bad was going on with the business. He decided to mention it to the Chief of Police next time he saw him.

Chapter Fourteen

The FBI "sneak and peek" team pulled their white panel van into the parking lot behind the Sheriff's office just after eleven PM. Locking up, they headed inside and after identifying themselves, were buzzed in and directed back to the conference room where Terry Rubin and two deputies were waiting. The three FBI agents didn't offer up a lot. Shook hands all around and introduced themselves as Josh, tall, thin, thirty something with longish wavy brown hair and a small bit of fuzz just below his lip; Randall, a little older, average size with short neat hair, which made him look more like an FBI agent in the classic sense; and Toby, average height, medium brown complexion, bald head and wary eyes, that seemed to take in everything around him at once. Terry introduced himself and his 2 Deputies, Carl Peters and Katy Wilson.

Introductions complete, they got right to business. Terry had been able to get the construction drawings for the

warehouse from the Durango Building
Department and he spread them out on the
table. At this point Josh took over and
opened them quickly to the electrical
pages. Toby started following
electrical, fire and burglar alarm
circuits with his finger, making notes on
his laptop as they went. Since most of
what they were saying sounded foreign to
the Deputies, tech speak, modulators and
transducers and other techy stuff, the
Deputies just sat back and let them work.

        While Josh and Toby worked over the
plans, Randall started setting up a
couple laptops and a few other pieces of
equipment that the deputies had never
seen before. In response to the
interested looks from the deputies,
Randall told them that if he explained it
to them, he would have to kill them.
Nervous chuckles all around.

        By one AM, it looked like the S & P
team was ready. They gathered everyone
around the table and Josh gave them a
rundown of what they hoped to accomplish.
Randall, it seemed, was the computer guru
and he would remain in the conference
room and would monitor the taps as the
others installed them. They were hoping
to pick up the phone and radio networks.
This would entail accessing the
electrical and security panels that
according to the plans were mounted on
the wall at the back of the building.
Outside the space. They would be using
the existing building circuitry to create

a net inside the space, basically turning
the entire building into one big phone
and voice tap. Anything said inside the
space or transmitted by any cell phone or
land line would be engulfed by the net
and would be transmitted instantly back
to Randall's computers. This was super
high tech and the nice thing about it was
that even if the bad guys swept the
building for listening devices, they
wouldn't find any.

At the same time Randall would be
attempting to locate any computers
connected to WIFI. He would be using
what he called a sniffer program to
filter out computers from all around the
area and attempt to isolate the ones that
were active inside the building. Terry
was amazed with what he was being told,
but he also imagined what this stuff
could do in the wrong hands. Scary. If
Randall could locate the computers, he
would hack into their systems, download
their files and activate their cameras.
Piece of cake.

They had also been instructed to
install GPS trackers on each trailer.
These were tiny little magnetic boxes
about the size of a cigarette lighter.
They would remain turned off so as not to
be detected. Once they were alerted to a
trailer moving, they would send a signal
to the box and activate the tracker.

Lastly, they would try to access
the roof, if possible, and attempt to

drop a couple cameras down the HVAC, heating ventilation and air conditioning ductwork, until they reached a diffuser that they might be able to drop into. Josh showed the deputies the cameras. Unreal. They were smaller than a pencil eraser but when Randall brought one up on the computer screen, the picture in Hi Def, was amazing. This would be the hardest part since the roof would probably make noise once someone stepped foot on it. If that failed, they would try to find another access point to follow.

The one piece they forgot to mention was that while all this was happening, the NSA had tasked a satellite to ping the building and they were now in the process of isolating any satellite transmission that might be coming from inside the building. This included SAT phones and laptops not connected to WIFI. They would piggy back a coded signature on each line they discovered, that they could then use to track the signal back to the other end. They would be able to do this no matter what kind of encryption the bad guys were using. This was technology so sophisticated that there were only a handful of people in the country that even knew it existed.

The S & P team gathered up their equipment and headed for the van. Terry and his two Deputies geared up and headed for Terry's unmarked unit. The two Deputies, both dressed completely in

black from head to toe, would position
themselves at either end of the fence
surrounding the truck yard since most of
the activity would take place at the back
of the building. Terry would take up his
overwatch position on the roof of the
auto body shop.

Chapter Fifteen

Terry did a final comm and sitrep check of the team and then gave the all clear. The S & P team, fully armed and dressed all in black looked like a couple ninjas as they raced across the parking lot behind the truck yard. This was where they would be the most exposed and everyone was on high alert. Once at the corner of the fence they pulled out an electric wrench and removed several of the bolts that tied the two fence corners together.

Opening a space large enough to squeeze through, they cleared the fence and knelt as low as they could and listened. Not hearing or seeing any movement, they raced across the grass and positioned themselves flat against the wall at the electrical panels. It only took a couple seconds to pick the lock on the electrical panel and the security system panel. Now Josh went to work with a bunch of wires and alligator clips and a monitor as he checked each circuit until he found the one he was looking

for. He then removed a small black box
from inside his jumpsuit, attached the
wires and slid the box down into a space
below the breakers where it wouldn't be
seen.

	At the same time Toby was doing the
same search on the security panel. At
one point he tapped Josh on the arm and
pointed to something in the box. Josh
nodded, and Toby proceeded to attach a
similar black box to the security panel.
After about five minutes of activity Josh
tapped his finger on the microphone
resting just under his chin.

	"We are connected to the security
and building electrical. Go ahead and run
a diagnostic and make sure we have a good
connection."

	Back at the office, Randall started
running his fingers over his keyboard,
like a machine. Then he would wait, check
a bunch of random numbers and move on to
the next test.

	"We are good. Reading five by five
on those lines."

	Josh began working on the cable
box, which fed the WIFI signal to the
building while Toby got out the tiny
cameras and headed down to the roof
ladder, that was conveniently located on
the side of the building. While Josh was
disconnecting the cable from the cable TV
provider and connecting in a signal
interceptor, Toby made a leap off the

ground and was able to catch the bottom
rung of the roof ladder located about
eight feet off the ground. He hung there
for just a second and then raced up the
ladder and stepped over the low parapet
wall.

Just then Terry sounded the alert.
"Guys, movement at the front door. I've
got one bad guy with a pistol coming out
the front door. He's looking around in
the air like he's checking the weather or
something. Hold tight."

Everyone froze. A minute later
Terry announced the all clear.

"I bet he was watching something on
cable when I disconnected the antennae.
He was probably checking to see if it was
windy or something, which might have
caused him to lose his signal."
Suggested Josh. "We are almost done
here."

Meanwhile on the roof, Toby had
found a conduit outside one of the air
conditioner unit, with some loose roofing
sealant around it and had fed a camera
down along it and was now watching the
picture on his phone to make sure he
could get a good view of the space. The
camera suddenly popped out into the open
and he had a view of the main garage
space. He slowly twisted the camera cord
looking for the best view and was stunned
when the view picked up a wall of fenced
off cells. There were 3 or 4 people
sleeping in each cell. It looked like a

prison. He counted eight such cells as he rotated the camera. Tapping the mike on the side of his head he asked Randall to check the camera feed. Randall responded that he had a good picture. Toby would have liked to get one more camera in the space, but he had already overshot the time they had allotted so he climbed back down the ladder and rejoined Josh.

They now headed around the front of the building, checked with Terry to make sure it was all clear and then ran along the row of trailers attaching a GPS tracker up under each trailer frame. Together they raced back to the corner of the fence and re-secured the chain link.

Josh reported that they were finished, and everyone headed back to their vehicles and returned to the office. Now they would just have to wait and see what the electronics revealed.

Chapter Sixteen

The morning following the visit by the attorney, a construction crew from a company Hector had never heard of showed up and starting loading materials from their truck into the loading dock. It seemed to Hector that they were unloading a lot of chain link fencing. He had no idea what they were planning.

The first thing the crew did was to start building a 2 X 4 wall separating four of the loading docks from the other two. They were efficient as hell and within 3 hours they had completely separated the two sections of the dock including installing a large man door with a very sophisticated electronic lock. They then turned their attention to the fencing and posts they had brought in and for the next 6 hours all anyone could hear was the drilling of concrete.

Claire tried to ask Hector what was going on but all she got from him was a shake of his head. Hector looked very uneasy, especially when he tried to ask the contractor what they were planning, and the lead worker refused to even answer him.

Dick arrived right in the middle of all the noise and walked right back out, not saying a word to anyone. He did not look pleased. Claire still had work to do so she contacted her drivers, answered calls from clients and continued arranging pickup and delivery schedules. Hector was no help and she just decided to stay out of whatever was going on. She liked her job, but she had been looking for a job when she found this one, so she wasn't too worried. At least not yet.

By midnight the construction crew was finished with whatever they were building on the other side of the new wall and disappeared as quickly as they had arrived. Hector had left long before the contractors finished and Claire left at six PM just like every night. Once the contractors left, everything seemed to return to normal, but that was far from the case.

When Claire arrived for work the next morning, Dick was already in the office and was in the process of brewing a pot of coffee. He offered her a cup and then poured one for himself.

"What do you think is going on, on the other side of the wall?" he asked her.

"I have no idea", she replied. "I hoped you would know. What's going on, Dick?"

"I'd rather not tell you at this point. Right now, nothing makes sense." With that Dick turned and headed towards his office and closed the door. End of discussion.

Hector arrived at his usual time, walked into the office said "Mornin", poured himself a cup of coffee and headed for his office. Claire thought to herself that this does not look good. Maybe it was time to look for another job.

Just as Claire was getting ready to head out the door for lunch a car pulled into the parking lot and parked in the "Visitors" space in front of the office door. Two men, a tall blond and a shorter Latino with a thick moustache got out of the car and walked in the door. Claire had never encountered anyone that she thought was menacing and she wasn't even sure she would recognize it if she did see it, but when these two approached the counter, she knew exactly what menacing meant and here it was looking over the counter at her.

"Help you gentlemen?" she inquired. It was obvious from their appearances that they were very well muscled and barely fit the suit jackets they were wearing.

"Tell Hector and Dick we are here to see them." Blondy smiled a sinister smile that sent a chill up Claire's back.

"Do you have an appointment?"

Moustache kind of sneered at her through two broken front teeth and said, "Never mind. We will find them ourselves." With that they turned and walked down the hall toward Dick and Hector's offices. Claire thought better of trying to stop them, so she got up from her desk, walked out the door and headed to her car. Lunch was waiting, somewhere, anywhere. She really didn't care. She just wanted out of the office.

Chapter Seventeen

Moustache pushed open Hector's office door and Hector almost pissed in his pants. He jumped up out of his chair, but Moustache held up his palm to indicate stop and then pointed towards the chair. Hector sat back down. Moustache stepped aside, and Dick walked in, or more like was pushed in, followed by Blondy. Dick was not so subtlety pointed toward one of the visitor chairs. Blondy took the other chair and Moustache stood in the doorway. This was intimidating, and Hector just looked at Dick who was looking at Moustache.

"Good afternoon gentlemen." Said Blondy. Blondy had a southern accent but it wasn't a smooth silky southern accent. His was harsh and sounded like he came from a very rural environment.

"We represent your new business partners and want to welcome you to our business family. We will be overseeing the operation in the space next door. We only have a few simple rules. One, stay out of our space. Two, don't ask questions and three, do not talk to anyone about our new business arrangement. If you can follow those simple rules, then we will get along fine, and we will all get rich. If you violate any one of those rules, then we will get rich and you and your family will get dead."

Blondy paused for dramatic effect and Dick squirmed uneasily in his chair. Hector just looked scared.

Blondy continued, "Now our employer wants this little venture to be a success and we will do whatever it takes to make it a success. We can do that without you if necessary, but we would prefer to keep everything looking as normal as possible, so let's all just agree right now to get along."

Hector nodded in agreement. Dick on the other hand started to speak up. Before Dick knew what was happening, he was lying on the floor next to the chair he had been sitting in moments ago. The stunned look on his face and the bright red mark on his cheek said it all.

Blondy merely turned sideways in his chair and looked at Dick siting on the floor. He glanced over his shoulder at Moustache, who just smiled that sinister smile. Blondy leaned forward.

"I guess I forgot to mention rule number four. Never try to voice your opinion to us. We don't care what you think or what you have to say. Now that was just an open hand slap. Next time I will break something. And by the way, my boss told me to make sure I tell you that if you ever tell him to shove his money up his ass again, we are going to have a serious problem and your family will not like the outcome. Understood?"

Hector looked at Dick and Dick looked at Blondy and they both shook their heads in agreement.

"Excellent." Blondy continued with a sneer on his face. "See, we are getting along already. This is going to be fun. So, you just keep running your operation and doing what you do, and we will take care of the rest."

With that Blondy got up from his chair and he and Moustache headed for the door.

Hector looked at Dick and said, "See I told you they had this place bugged."

Dick looked at Hector and didn't say a word, just headed back to his office rubbing his cheek. He never even saw Blondy move his hand, but it sure hurt like hell. He hadn't been hit like that since his old man beat him when he was a senior in high school and he had backtalked his mother. Inside he was steaming. He didn't know what he would need to do to take care of these guys,

but he was starting to get mad and when
he got mad he was unpredictable.

Chapter Eighteen

Buck and Terry sat across the table from "Scratch" in interview room one. Outside the window of the interview room stood Sheriff Sinclair, Christine Brewer, the District Attorney, and Jess Gonzales from the DEA. "Scratch" was coming down off the high he was on when Terry arrested him and squirmed in his seat. Buck offered him a cup of coffee or something to drink and then asked Terry to remove the handcuffs. "Scratch" rubbed his wrists and looked at Buck nervously.

"Scratch", my name is Buck Taylor and I am an agent with the Colorado Bureau of Investigation and I would like to hear the story you told Deputy Terry, here. Can you repeat it for me?"

"Scratch" started scratching at the scabs on his right arm and looked around the room like he was trying to find the story is his drug addled mind. Finally, it looked like his brain engaged and he began telling Buck a story.

"Dem Mexicans have taken over Hector's place and they scarin the shit out a people. They got them kids all locked up in cages like it's the damn zoo and they only let them out to do they drug sorten and packin." His mind started to drift. "Some dem little chickitas are pretty sweet lookin, but I never touch any of them. Ain't lookin for no trouble with the blond boss. He wackier than a crazy old coot and meaner an a snake." Scratch stared at the ceiling.

"And you have seen these people in the cages yourself?" Buck asked.

"Sho have." Replied Scratch. His brain engaged again. "I was over they heppin load one of the truck for Hector. He gives me a couple bucks to load trucks sometimes. I asked him what was behind the new wall, but he wouldn't say so, when he wasn't lookin and the blond guy came out the door I snuck in to get a peek. The kids was all stuffin pills in toys and putting em back in boxes like dey was new." He stopped again and just stared. Terry asked him if he was OK. Click, brain engaged. "I didn't steal no drugs. Dem pills was just lyin on the table and I was gonna go talk to one dem sweet chickitas, but then the Boss come back in the door and I grabbed a handful of pills en high tailed it for the back door. That was when I seen dem cages." Click, brain disengaged.

Buck looked at Terry, who tapped on "Scratch's" hand. That seemed to bring him back. Click, brain engaged.

"Did you ask Hector what was going on after you took the pills?"

"Nope. Ain't been back there. Scared Blondy might get me. Figured I'd sell dem pills and maybe go to Ignacio and party. Ain't been to Ignacio in a while. Knew this girl there once. Might look her up and…."

""Scratch" focus." Buck raised his voice a notch or two. "Who else might know about the drugs, anyone you know?"

"Scratche's" brain was rapidly heading south. He looked at the ceiling again. Buck was about to give up.

"Claire probly knows. She knows everything. She always been nice to me. Gives me money when I got no drugs to sell so I can eat. She not happy now." Click, Brain disengaged for the last time.

Buck got up and the Sheriff buzzed the door to let him out while Terry put the handcuffs back on "Scratch" and turned him over to one of the jail deputies.

Jess looked at Buck. "Guy sure has a way with words. Wonder how many pills he sampled. Should make a great witness."

Buck looked at Sheriff Sinclair. "Who is this Claire he mentioned. She real or imaginary?"

"Oh, she's real. She's the Office Manager. We go to the same church, but I haven't seen her much lately. You think she could help?"

"Let's get her address and see what she has to say. It's risky. If she is part of this, we could blow the whole case. I think we should also talk to some of their regular drivers. They may not be in on the deal and might be a good source."

Terry said he would get Claire's address and track down one or two of the local drivers.

Christine Brewer didn't look happy. "Buck, we don't have a lot to go on. This "witness" is pretty much worthless. If we don't get something back from the electronics, we may not have a case. Let me know if you need anything. I need to get to court." She left the office with a worried look on her face.

Jess chimed in. "She's right. We have our necks out a long way on this and we may not have anything to go on."

"Look Jess." Said Buck. "We all know something big is going on. Maybe we need to shake the bushes a little. I'm thinking we should try to talk to this Hector and Dick, someplace away from their warehouse. Maybe we can get something from them or at least push them to make a move. I have it on good authority that Dick has been talking in his beer and he doesn't sound like someone making a big score. More the opposite."

"OK." Jess said. "But let's do this soon. We have a shit load of resources sitting on their asses." Jess headed out the door.

Sheriff Sinclair looked at Terry and Buck. "She's right. If we needed a warrant with what we have, we wouldn't get one. I'll talk to the sneak and peek team in a little bit and see what they have. In the meantime, why don't you to go talk to Claire Ringsby. The Sheriff left the room.

Chapter Nineteen

The first two delivery trucks arrived after midnight a couple nights after the construction crew completed their work and pulled up to the loading dock doors. Blondy and Moustache opened the loading dock door, and with the help of the three guards who had arrived the day before, silently and quickly offloaded the workers they had smuggled in from Mexico to sort and package the drugs. When he opened the back door of the first trailer he was met by a sea of young scared faces. Thirty in all.

The young people, mostly girls except for 10 young men had all been kidnapped by the cartel. The cartel had put out word in the neighboring towns that they were looking for young laborers to work in the fields harvesting crops. When the young people showed up seeking those jobs they were immediately grabbed up and locked away in a warehouse in the middle of the desert. Their phones and other electronic devices were taken from them and their contact with the outside world was extinguished.

Over the next couple weeks the young people had been drugged and abused. They were tortured until their will to escape had completely disappeared. Some of the young girls had been repeatedly raped. Even though their families had looked for them and had contacted the local authorities, no sign of the group was ever found. The cartel had done a thorough job of making these folks disappear without a trace.

Now, here they were in a foreign place in the middle of the night being herded into cages like animals. They had no idea of the date or the time or where they were, and they had no idea if they would still be alive tomorrow morning. Violence was their only reward for working sometime eighteen-hour days, with just enough food to sustain them.

The ride in the back of the hot stuffy trailer had taken 12 hours. The guards had come in just as they were finishing the meal of empty tortillas and a bottle of water and hustled them into a couple smaller panel trucks. The trucks had no windows, so again, no reference of where they were. Two hours later they arrived at a larger warehouse. This time they were given a bottle of water each and a couple rice cakes and put in the back of the trailer. Inside, the trailer was filled with metal cots with

mattresses so thin you could almost see
through them and some boxes filled with
clothes. They were told to sit down and
be quiet or they would be beaten, or
worse.

It was a long hot drive and at one
point they had stopped for a few minutes.
They all thought they might have a chance
to get out and stretch their legs or use
a restroom instead of the two buckets
that had been left with them, but that
didn't happen. A few minutes later they
were back on the road and they settled in
for whatever awaited them.

During the long ride, several of
the young people got sick from the heat
and the movement of the trailer and after
a few hours in the heat and stuffiness of
the trailer, the space became almost
unbearable due to the smell. The longer
they went the hotter and more putrid it
got.

The trailer finally came to a stop
and when the doors were opened they drank
in the fresh air. Then they saw
Moustache and Blondy and all their fears
returned. Blondy at least had a little
bit of a compassionate side. Moustache
was just brutal and he seemed to really
enjoy it. Back at the first place they
stayed Moustache never thought twice
about picking out one of the prettier
girls and taking her back to his office.
The others would hear the screams of
anguish coming from the office but there

was nothing they could do but try to console that person when she returned.

Moustache also liked the young men, but not for sexual pleasure. He seemed to enjoy using them as punching bags and if Moustache wasn't satisfied by the young girl he took to his office he always found a young man to take it out on. Blondy would just watch and smile that sadistic smile.

It had taken a couple weeks but Moustache and Blondy and their helpers managed to break the spirits of everyone in the group. Eventually, there were no more tears, only the sad acceptance that this was to be their lives and that maybe someday they would be freed. They no longer thought about family or friends. They only cared about making it through another day alive and getting their next pill. Although the reality was that many of them would have preferred to be dead than to live like this.

Chapter Twenty

The young folks had no idea where they were, but they knew they were not near home anymore. The air seemed thinner and was a little cooler which was very much appreciated after the torturous trip they had just endured. The new space looked fresh and clean and did not smell of human waste and excrement like the old place did. Moustache gathered them around at the entrance to the cage and told them in Spanish that this would be their new home for a while and if they performed their tasks without any problems they would be released soon to return to their families. Many of these kids had grown up on the streets and had no recollection of families.

He continued on, telling them that they could use the restroom that was contained within the cage area and when they weren't working they were to remain in their cages. If they broke any of the rules punishment would be swift and painful. They were not to go outside the loading dock door without a guard and they were not to go through the door that was at the other end of the warehouse. Most importantly, if they were told to be quiet, they were to do exactly that, or they would be dealt with severely.

He gave them ten minutes to use the restroom and then they were to start removing the furniture and clothing from the trailer and setting up their cages. Once the trailer was empty and the cages set up, they were to start unloading the other trailer. They would have to hurry if they wanted to get any sleep, but work would start bright and early the next morning.

The young folks worked quickly, removing the crates from the back of the second truck. The idea of getting some sleep was on all their minds. Once the crates were all arranged in the middle of the floor, Blondy gave them permission to get a few hours sleep. They all headed off to the cages, except for Maria. Moustache had personally broken Maria and he enjoyed her a lot. She was spunky and had some spirit and the fact that she was only sixteen didn't concern him in the least. He grabbed her by the arm and pulled her toward the guard's office.

Blondy looked over and said. "Hey man. Why don't you let her get some sleep? She has to work in the morning."

Moustache looked over at him and smiled that toothless smile. "Damn you bro. She is going to work now." He laughed a wicked little laugh and slammed the door. Moustache was not quiet in the pursuit of his pleasures and the guards finally went and stood outside so they didn't have to hear what was going on.

Blondy actually hated the little cretin but he was a favorite of the boss and Blondy was getting paid good money for this gig, so he just walked away. After a while the noise level dropped and Blondy and three of the guards headed to the little motel they were staying at about 10 miles outside of town on the way to Mancos. Moustache and the other two guards would take the first night's watch, at least what was left of it.

The young folks were roused from what little sleep they had been able to get. They were given a few minutes to wash up and use the restroom and then they assembled for breakfast. Moustache had a couple of the girls prepare breakfast in the new kitchen area that was installed next to the cages. It wasn't much: just a refrigerator, stove and some shelves and a counter. The young folks didn't care, for the first time in a long time they had a decent meal. The girls had cooked scrambled eggs and beans and that was piled on tortillas. This was almost like heaven, if heaven were a prison. There was even coffee for those who wanted it.

Blondy returned just as breakfast was wrapping up and gave them their

orders in Spanish. They were told to get
the work tables set up that they had
unloaded from the truck and to start
sorting the pills into piles, just like
they had been shown to do at their last
place. The toys for the second part of
the job would arrive by the end of the
day and then they could start the
assembly process. They knew they would
be watched very carefully and taking
pills off the table would result in a
severe beating.

And this is how their day would go
until the next truck arrived. They would
be fed a second meal towards the end of
the day and then locked in their cages
for the night. This is how every day
would go with only the hope of being
released.

Chapter Twenty One

Buck grabbed a bottle of Coke from the cooler in the lunchroom and went looking for Terry Rubin. He knew Terry had a long night with the "sneak and peek" so he wasn't sure if he was in yet. He found Terry sitting at his desk. Terry had his feet up and a cup of coffee in his hand. He looked so contemplative that Buck almost hated to disturb him.

"Morning." Said Buck. "Were you able to get any sleep last night?"

"Yeah, a little", replied Terry. He put his feet on the floor and sat up, setting his coffee down on the desk. "Those guys were really amazing last night. They were quick, quiet and efficient as hell. They told me they thought they had everything they needed. They are monitoring from the conference room."

Buck looked at the mess of files on Terry's desk and wondered to himself how this young guy got anything accomplished with such a disorganized manner. Buck had always been meticulous in how he kept the files from an investigation and even last night he had spent several hours in his hotel room assembling his investigation notebook. This would eventually be the work product that would put Carlos Rojas and his cartel away for life.

"Were you able to get Claire Ringsby's address?" Buck asked.

"Right here." Replied Terry. "She lives in a rental half way down East 4th Avenue, between East 4th and East 5th Streets. You want me to come along?" Terry handed Buck a slip of paper with the address written on it.

"No, I have this. What I would like you to do is track down one of the drivers we talked about and see if we can get someone to talk out of school."

Buck turned and headed towards the door but was stopped just as he got there by Sheriff Sinclair. "Oh, Buck. Glad I caught you. The "sneak and peek" team has started downloading computer files and they have already recorded a couple sat phone conversations. The FBI sent two computer analysts down this morning to help decipher the computer stuff. A lot of it is encrypted. NSA is attempting to break the encryption. Should have something we can look at in a couple hours."

"That's great", replied Buck. Text me when they have it together. I am heading out to see if I can find Claire Ringsby and then I might see if I can find either Dick or Hector and have a conversation."

"OK," said the Sheriff. "You want any back up?"

"No. Hopefully this is just a conversation. By the way, I asked Terry Rubin to track down one of the drivers and see if we get anything with that approach. See you later." Buck walked out the back door and headed for his car.

Leaving the Sheriff's office parking lot, he headed back out to US 550 and headed north. At College Drive, he turned right until he got to East 4th Avenue and headed south past East 5th Street and found the address Terry had given him in the middle of the block on the right side. It was a small well-kept little ranch with a cute front porch and a separate garage that sat behind the house. A row of roses was in full bloom along a small picket fence that fronted the sidewalk. Buck turned off the engine and sat for a minute, contemplating his approach. He hoped this was not a huge mistake. He had a sense from his conversation with the snitch, if the snitch could be believed, that the two owners and the Office Manager might not be willing participants in this whole thing. If he was wrong, then his visit to Claire Ringsby was going to be a colossal mistake. He decided to just be straight up front with her and see where it went.

He opened the car door and stepped out realizing too late that it would be obvious to anyone who might be watching Claire's house that he was a cop. His badge was clipped to his belt and he carried a two tone Kimber 45 caliber Ultra Carry pistol in a DiSantos brown leather holster in his waist band. Since this was July, he didn't have a coat or vest on to conceal the gun, so he decided, to hell with it, he would have to take a chance that she was not being watched.

He crossed the street and pushed open the little white picket gate and walked up the front walk. As he approached the porch he noticed that the door was open. He slowed his pace and unsnapped the thumb break on his holster and rested his right hand on his gun. He walked up the steps to the porch and looked through the open front door. Stepping across the threshold he called out.

"Claire Ringsby." He waited but received no response. "Ms. Ringsby, my name is Buck Taylor and I am with the Colorado Bureau of Investigation. Are you in there?"

Just then a little old lady stuck her head out of a door halfway down the hall. She looked a little nervous.

"Can I help you young man?" she said.

Buck smiled. He hadn't been a young man in a long time.

"Yes Ma'am. I am looking for Claire Ringsby. Is that you by chance?"

"Heavens no", relied the little old lady. "I'm Martha Davidson. I own this house. What do you want with Claire if I might ask?"

"Ma'am. My name is Buck Taylor and I am an investigator with the Colorado Bureau of Investigations and I was told that Claire Ringsby was living here."

Mrs. Davidson stepped out of what Buck assumed was a bathroom and pulled off a pair of pink rubber gloves. She approached the front door and asked if Buck had any ID. Buck pointed to his badge on his belt and pulled his cred pack from his back pocket, opened it and showed her his CBI ID card.

"Sorry officer. My late husband told me to never be too careful. He was an accountant. A very meticulous man, but it paid off because he left me in good shape after he passed."

Buck smiled as he put away his ID. "Does Claire still live here?"

Mrs. Davidson replied. "She did until yesterday. Got a voicemail from her yesterday morning saying she was leaving town and I shouldn't worry about the security deposit because she was in a hurry. Came over here this morning to talk to her but she was already gone. Left everything here except her clothes from the looks of it. Don't know what I am going to do with all her furniture. Guess I can rent it out as "Furnished." Fifteen years she lived here, and she didn't even leave a forwarding address. Tried her phone but it went straight to voice mail. I hate talking on those things so I didn't leave a message."

"Ma'am. Would you mind if I came in and looked around?"

"Don't you need some kind of warrant or something to do that, officer?"

"No Ma'am. As long as I have your permission, it's OK."

Mrs. Davidson thought about it for a minute and said. "Well I guess it's OK, you being a cop and all. Come on in."

Chapter Twenty Two

Buck stepped into the entry foyer which was not much bigger than a coat closet. The house was set up like a typical old 4 square house. A living room and small kitchen on one side and a small dining room, a bathroom and one bedroom on the other side of a narrow hallway. Someone over the years had added a second bedroom in an addition off the back of the house. Buck noticed that the house was nicely painted, had beautiful woodwork built-ins, moldings and awesome dark stained hardwood floors. All in all, a very nice little house. Mrs. Davidson went back to cleaning.

Buck walked into each room and scanned them with the eye of a seasoned investigator. Looking for anything that seemed out of place or amiss. He had no idea what if anything he was looking for but he would know it if he found it. He didn't find it in the living room or in the kitchen. The dining room was set up with a table and four chairs and a small cupboard that contained a set of

dinnerware and glasses. He found nothing
of interest in the drawers in the
cupboard.

        Mrs. Davidson was still working in
the bathroom, so he just glanced in as he
walked by. Didn't see anything of
interest and walked into the bedroom.
The first thing he noticed was that the
bed was made. If Claire Ringsby had been
taken against her will, he doubted the
bad guys would let her make the bed
first. The closets and drawers in the
dresser were all empty as well.

        Buck headed for the back bedroom
which it appeared Claire had used as an
office and workout room. There was a
small desk. No computer. A yoga mat was
lying on the floor and a couple small
five-pound weights sat next to it. Not
much to see. As he was stepping out of
the bedroom a thought occurred to him and
he stepped over to the bathroom door.

        "Mrs. Davidson. Did you find any
trash in any of the trash cans when you
got here this morning?"

        Mrs. Davidson stopped cleaning the
toilet and looked up. "There was trash
in the kitchen can and in the back
bedroom by the desk. Not much. I threw
it in the cans out back by the garage."

        "Thank you, Ma'am." Buck turned to
head out the back door towards the
garage.

Mrs. Davidson stood at the back door as he went and said, "You know, officer. If you're not doing anything later, there's a dance at the Grange Hall tonight. Might be fun."

"Thanks for the offer Ma'am but I have a lot to do." Buck continued along the walkway.

"You might find my expertise enjoyable." Mrs. Davidson said with a sly and slightly naughty smile. Buck waved his hand over his head and opened the garage door. The trash cans were lined up along the back wall of the garage. Other than those, the rest of the garage was totally empty. Who lives like this, thought Buck, thinking back to his own garage in Gunnison that was probably a mess right now.

Buck opened the first trash can and found it empty. The second one contained a small bag of trash. Buck turned the lid upside down, placed it on the floor and dumped the bag's contents onto the overturned lid. It was mostly paper stuff: tissues, napkins, an empty McDonald's bag and a drink cup. He almost missed the small slip of paper that was stuck to the wet side of the cup. He could barely make out the words, but it looked like it said United, with today's date, the number 275 and the time of 5:50PM.

Claire Ringsby was running.

Buck pulled out his cell phone and called the Sheriff.

The Sheriff answered on the first ring. "Buck, I was just getting ready to call you. We have a body."

Buck stopped short. "What? A body? Where?"

"About 20 miles north of town in a culvert. Couple hikers found it."

"OK", Buck replied. "I am on my way. You got forensics on the way?"

"Forensics just got here. What did you need?" the Sheriff asked.

'Oh, right. Can you get one of your people to write up a Material Witness warrant for Claire Ringsby and get a judge to sign it. She's in the wind and I think she is catching a flight today, but I don't know from where."

"Done. Get here soon as you can. Straight up 550. You can't miss us."

Buck headed out the driveway, mostly to avoid Mrs. Davidson, taking the little slip of paper with him. As he got in his car he dialed the Director's cell phone.

"Buck. I hear you have a body. Is it related to the drug thing?" No one still ever says, hello. Word also travels way too fast sometimes.

"Don't know yet sir, I am on my way. I need a little help sir." Buck explained the scrap of paper he found at Claire Ringsby's house and that the Sheriff was putting together a witness warrant. He then asked the Director if he could get someone to contact the airline or TSA or whomever, and see where that flight was leaving from. It could be Denver, it could be Albuquerque or hell, it could even be Salt Lake City or Phoenix. If Claire left last night she could have reached any of those places by now.

The Director told him he would take care of it and he would call him back as soon as he knew. He told Buck to let him know what he found at the body site. The Director hung up. Seems like no one says goodbye anymore either. Buck disconnected, did a three-point turn in the street, headed back up to College Avenue, jumped on 550 and headed north. Once clear of the city he flipped on the blue and red flashers that were buried in the car's grill and dropped the hammer.

Chapter Twenty Three

Dick Dillon wasn't sure what he was going to do. If this was all for real then he was going to get paid a lot of money to keep his mouth shut about what was going on at the tucking company. He hated the idea that someone could just waltz in and take over a business that he and Hector had worked so hard to develop. He hated even more the idea that they were somehow working for a Mexican cartel. He feared for his family and he feared for his workers, especially Claire Ringsby. She had been with the company since the beginning. She took a chance right from the start that she might not get paid or paid on time since starting a trucking company was not an easy deal.

Over the years Dick had always tried to help Claire out if she needed help. Money, time off. He did what he could. She was awesome at her job and kept the company humming like a well-oiled machine. She never missed a day of work. Never complained about the hours or the job and she got along great with

the clients and the drivers. She was
great to have around. Now she was right
in the middle of their mess and it wasn't
fair.

     Dick picked up the note that Hector
had given him with his offshore bank
account number on it, picked up the phone
and dialed the bank. He had no idea
where the bank was, but it really didn't
matter. After he identified himself, the
person he spoke with helped him set up
the new account and transfer the money he
wanted moved over. He had never dealt
with that kind of money and was a little
nervous, but the person on the other end
of the phone made it all seamless. He
hung up and for the first time in a
couple weeks felt good about himself.

     Whatever he decided to do was one
thing, but he had an obligation to Claire
as well. She didn't ask for any of this
and he was worried for her safety. He
had walked into her office one day and
caught Moustache leering at her and it
bothered him a lot. He finally made a
decision and he got up and headed toward
Claire's office. When he got to her desk
he put his finger up to his lips to
signal her to be quiet and then pointed
towards the front door. He wanted her to
follow him.

     Once outside, Dick looked around to
make sure no one was watching. He moved
closer to Claire.

"I have bad feeling about everything that is going on around here and think you should make plans to get out of town before something happens."

Claire looked at him confused. "Are we in danger?"

Dick and Hector had never told Claire the whole story of what was going on, but she had a pretty good idea that what was going on wasn't good and was probably illegal in some way. She had already considered leaving. She liked her job and she liked working for Dick and Hector, but her imagination had started to run away on her. And she really didn't like Blondy or his friend.

She started to object. "Dick, my life is here. I can't just…"

"Look I am worried about what's going to happen once these guys decide they don't need us around. I am working on a plan for my family and I want to help you get out. I want you to book a flight out of Denver for as soon as you can get there. Maybe go visit the family in Vermont. That would be good. Clear out of your house and just go."

"Dick. I can't afford to just walk away from everything in my life."

Dick replied. "I took care of that for you. I set up an account in an offshore bank and transferred fifty grand into an account in your name."

He handed her a slip of paper with an account number written on it and the name of the bank. Claire was stunned.

"I can't take your money", she said.

"Yes, you can. Its money from them and I don't care about it. Take it and run. These guys have a long reach so keep a low profile. Finish out the day so no one is the wiser and then make your arrangements and go. Don't tell anyone where you are going. You're a nice lady Claire, and I have enjoyed working with you these many years, but I don't want to see you again after today. Stay safe."

Before she could respond, Dick headed for his car, hopped in and pulled out of the lot. Claire's life had just taken a strange turn and she was more scared now than she was before. She headed back inside to try to finish her day. Her life was about to change in ways she couldn't even imagine.

Chapter Twenty Four

Terry Rubin and Deputy Danny Silvio left the Sheriff's Office parking lot and headed for 550. Turning north, they made a right at East 15th St, which turned into Florida Road and eventually turned left onto Folsom Place, which led them to the parking lot at Folsom Park. Terry had asked Danny to change out of his uniform so they would not attract attention when they went to see Franky Fortuna.

Danny and Franky were high school friends and had stayed in touch over the years. It was Danny's call to Franky's house that led the two Deputies to Folsom Park. Franky was one of the four regular drivers that worked for Colorado Overland Transportation. According to his wife, today was his day off so he had taken their son over to the park to practice batting and catching. Franky's son was in his first year of Little League and they tried to practice whenever they could.

Terry parked the car and the Deputies scanned the park, finally Danny pointed to the baseball diamond. The Deputies were hoping they wouldn't spook Franky, but they still decided to approach together.

Walking across the grass toward home plate, Danny called out. "Hey Franky." And gave a little wave. Franky turned and placing his hand over his eyes to block some of the sun, he stared to see who was calling him. Recognizing Danny, he waved back. He didn't recognize the guy he was with.

Franky told his son to hold the ball for a minute and walked toward the two men.

"Yo Danny. What's up?" He asked.

Danny and Terry closed the gap and Danny and Franky shook hands.

"Franky, this is Terry Rubin. We work together. Terry was wondering if he could ask you a couple questions?" Danny said.

Franky looked a little leery. "Sure. What's this about?"

Terry hadn't really come up with a game plan on the way over to the park, so he decided to just play it straight and gauge Franky's reaction.

"Franky, we have been hearing stories about some strange things going on over at Colorado Overland and I am trying to see what's real and what's not."

Franky looked a little puzzled at first and then a look of concern came over his face. He tried to fake his way through it.

"I'm not sure what you're talkin about. I just drive for them. Don't have anything to do with the business."

Terry wasn't biting. "Look Franky, we can keep this real friendly so as not to concern your son or we can slap the cuffs on you and haul your ass down to the office and do this more formally. I'm willing to take this in whatever direction you want to go, but if you lie to me again, we are going to have a problem."

Franky glanced over his shoulder at his son standing at home plate. He gave him a little wave to show him everything was OK and turned back towards Terry.

"Look", he said. "I don't want to see anything happen to my family. They got everybody at the shop scared. You got to keep me out of this."

Danny said. "I'm gonna leave you to it. I'll be over by your son. Take your time. We'll be OK for a few minutes."

"OK Franky." Said Terry. "We will do all we can to keep you out of this. At this point we are just having a friendly conversation in a park. Don't make me regret this."

Franky could see that Terry was serious, so he decided it was in his best interest to be as straight as possible.

"We don't really know what's go on, me and the other drivers. Suddenly, this past month, they blocked off two-thirds of the warehouse and we are not allowed in that space. We have been handling our regular deliveries but there are nine more trucks and nine trailers in the yard. Our business has been good but not that good. That's a big investment."

Terry let him continue.

"We can hear people working next door, but we never see anybody and since we are on the road we are kind of out of the loop."

"I heard from someone that the bosses went after each other a couple weeks back. No one knows why but the rumor is they have a new partner. Big money and a lot of business. One of the other drivers said that he tried to ask one of the new loaders what was going on and a big blond guy came out and told him to mind his damn business."

"Any talk about drugs or illegals being in the place?" Terry asked.

"Nah. Nothing like that but I can tell from talking to Claire, the office lady, that she seems to be kind of scared all the time. What's going on?"

Terry explained. "Right now, we are just looking into some stories we've heard, so we are not sure what's going on. Any indication that any of the other regular drivers are working with this new partner?"

"I doubt it. Everyone I spoke to seemed just as concerned as me. We just wondering if we gonna have a pay check next month."

Terry thought for a minute and said. "If you hear anything new, you give Danny a call and he will get your message to me, OK? And don't let anyone know we were talking."

Franky asked. "This all sounds pretty serious. We are all a little scared but are we in danger? I got a family, man."

"Just be cool. You will be alright. You see a problem, you reach out right away. OK?"

Terry waved at Danny, who handed the ball back to Franky's son and headed over to Terry. As he passed Franky, he said. "Hey man, you need anything give me a call. You and Terry cool?"

"Yeah, I think we are good. Thanks."

Danny caught up to Terry and was just about to ask if he got what he needed when Terry's phone rang.

"Terry." He said as he listened to the caller.

"OK. Let the boss know we are on the way."

Terry hung up and looked at Danny. "Looks like we got a body up by Cascade Creek. We need to head that way."

Terry and Danny jogged to Terry's car. Hopped in. Terry hit the flashers and headed out the park, back down Florida Road and turned right onto 550. Once on the highway he hit the gas.

Chapter Twenty Five

Buck spotted the flashing lights farther up the hill, just as he passed the entrance into the Purgatory ski area. As he approached the scene, he had to pull past the turn for County 591, because the road was full of emergency vehicles. He pulled over on the side of the road. Just as he was about to get out of the car his phone rang.

Buck checked the caller ID and answered the call.

"Yes Sir?" He asked.

"Have you gotten to the body scene yet?" asked Director Jackson.

"Just pulling up now."

"Good" replied the Director. I just got off the phone with our tech guys. United Flight 275 leaves DIA at 5:50 tonight. We checked the passenger list. Don't ask me how. There is a Claire Ringsby travelling tonight to LaGuardia Airport in New York City. Do you have the witness warrant yet?"

"I will check with the Sheriff as soon as I can find her. Do we have someone who can intercept her at the airport?"

"I do. I have Tracy and Doonen enroute to the airport now. They will hook up with Denver Police once they get there and then go grab her before she gets on the plane. I was going to have them handle the interview at the airport to save time. Anything specific you want to know? I have already briefed them about what you have going on."

"Thanks boss. They should be able to handle this without me. I see the Sheriff up ahead. I will call you right back."

Buck disconnected the call and as he went to put his phone back in his pocket it rang again. This time it was Terry Rubin. "Buck, did you get the word that we have a body?"

"Yeah" replied Buck. "I just got to the site. Where are you?"

"Just passing Purgatory. We can see the lights."

"Good," Buck replied. "I need to find the Sheriff. Let's talk when you get here."

Buck disconnected his phone and put it away as he headed towards the yellow crime tape. As he got to the tape he presented his ID to the Deputy who was responsible for logging in all the people on the scene. He let Buck pass under the tape.

Buck walked up to the Sheriff who was standing just at the top of the ravine talking to two guys in plain clothes. As he approached, the Sheriff stopped talking.

"Hi Buck", she said. "Buck, these are my two homicide guys, Detectives Quinn and Romero. Guys, this is Buck Taylor, CBI."

Buck looked at the two homicide detectives. They looked like homicide detectives you would find in any law enforcement office in the country. He had worked with dozens of guys over the years who looked just like them. Quinn was probably Buck's age and was most likely the lead. He was about five-ten, two hundred and forty pounds, with a gut that hung over his belt from too many well cooked meals. He wore a light grey suit with a wide tie. He had the knot pulled down a couple inches and his top button was unbuttoned. Buck figured his shirt collar had probably gotten a little too tight to keep buttoned. What little hair he still had was plastered to his head from the heat.

Romero was Hispanic and quite a bit younger than Quinn. He wore blue jeans and a short sleeve button down shirt with the top two buttons open. He had a thick moustache and curly black hair. His dark eyes didn't stop moving during the entire introduction, like he was constantly looking for something. Buck figured he had good observations skills. In his hand he held an HP tablet and was entering information as he was introduced. Buck shook hands with both men. Quinn's handshake was strong but damp. Romero's was firm and dry.

The Sheriff looked at Quinn. "Please fill Buck in on what we have so far."

He was about to start when Terry Rubin and Danny Silvio crossed under the crime scene tape and signed in with the deputy with the clipboard. Then walked over to where Buck, the Sheriff and the two detectives stood. Buck held up his hand to Quinn, signaling him to wait just a second.

As they arrived the detectives exchanged pleasantries with Terry and Danny. The formalities over, Buck asked Quinn to start. Quinn started the debrief with a strong voice.

"The deceased appears to be Hispanic male. About five feet four to five feet six. His weight looks a little light for his height. Cause of death appears to be a slit throat. From what we could see the cut seems to be clean and deep. The Forensic Pathologist will let us know more. The Doc estimates time of death to be forty-eight to seventy-two hours ago. The body does not appear to have been killed here. Maybe just dumped. Soon as the Doctor is done, forensics will start documenting the scene and we will look for evidence. The Doc did say that the body had been badly beaten prior to death."

Quinn checked his notes on the little pad he carried. Buck figured he wasn't much into technology. He looked over at Romero. Romero looked at his tablet and continued.

"Body was found at 11:30 by two hikers who had been out on a day hike from the resort. They hadn't noticed the body when they started out this morning, but they said they weren't really looking. Something caught their eye as they were coming back. They think it might have been a flash from the sun hitting his belt buckle at just the right angle. As Mark said, no ID that we could find. First deputy on the scene called it in right away and started taping off a perimeter. The body is not located in an easy place to get to. Wasn't placed carefully as far as we can tell. Maybe just thrown off the side of the road. If you look over there, just above the pathology tech, you can see a lot of broken branches leading to the culvert. Since it didn't rain yesterday or today we can't determine when it was dropped. We told the Doc that the victim appeared to have a streak of something white on his shirt. The tech took a field sample."

Romero stopped, looked at his tablet and appeared a little uncertain as to where to go next.

"Nice report guys." Said Buck. "Thanks."

He signaled for the Sheriff and Terry to follow him and left the two detectives talking to Silvio.

"Anything that connects this to our guys?" Buck asked.

The Sheriff replied. "The first deputy on the scene was one of the deputies who was working with Terry on the surveillance. He is the one who took pictures of the guy who threw the toy over the fence before he got grabbed by one of the guards. He didn't get too close to the body, but he swears it looks like the guy from the pictures. The Forensic Pathologist has the pictures down there with him to see if we can get a comparison."

"Ok, good. By the way, were you able to get the Material Witness Warrant?" Buck asked.

The Sheriff said. "Oh, I almost forgot. Yes, we have it in the office, signed by the judge. Where do you want it?"

Buck reached into his pocket and handed her a card with a phone number with a 303 area code on it. He asked her if she could have someone fax the warrant

to this number. He told her about the
phone call with the Director just before
he arrived and that they were waiting for
the warrant to go in and grab Claire
Ringsby. The Sheriff stepped away and
made a phone call. Spoke a few words,
read the number off the card, hung up and
handed the card back to Buck.

"Done", she said.

Buck pulled out his phone, stepped
away and called the Director. The
Director answered on the second ring.

Before the Director could speak,
Buck said, 'Director, the warrant should
be coming through on the fax line now, so
we should be good on Claire Ringsby,"

"Anything on the body?" the
Director interrupted.

Buck explained what they knew so
far and that they were waiting for the
Forensic Pathologist to give them the all
clear on the site. He would call back as
soon as he had anything.

Chapter Twenty Six

Blondy was furious. Even Moustache had never seen him this mad. If it was possible for a human to explode, then this would have been that moment. The Mexican kid was lying on the floor in a ball. When the guard brought him back into the warehouse, Blondy had proceed to beat the kid mercilessly. He hit and kicked him multiple times in the head and gut with his balled-up fist. Hard enough that the young folks who were working on the production line thought he was dead.

Blondy finally stopped beating on the unconscious kid and turned. Gritting his teeth, he looked at the guard who was supposed to be watching the door. "How the hell did you let this asshole get out the door?"

The guard looked like he wasn't sure if he should answer the question or not. He just looked down at the ground. This made Blondy even madder and before the guard knew what was happening Blondy hit him full force in the face, busting his nose and breaking off a couple teeth. The guard hit the ground hard. Everyone stopped what they were doing. Not knowing what would happen next.

Blondy reached down and grabbed the guard and with one big hand on his throat, lifted him off the ground and pushed him against the wall. The guard was a pretty good size guy. A former Mexican Federal Police Officer who knew how to dish out pain, yet Blondy was able to lift him up with one arm so that his feet were dangling three inches off the ground. Blondy looked him dead in the eye and with that sadistic sneer said, "If you ever let one of these kids escape again, I will cut your balls off and feed them to you. DO YOU UNDERSTAND?"

The guard didn't answer, so with his other hand Blondy pulled a twelve-inch KA-Bar knife out of the sheath hanging from his belt and pushed against the zipper on the guard's pants. The guard's eyes got as big as saucers.

Repeating each word, slowly for emphasis, Blondy repeated the question. "Do…You…understand?"

The guard answered this time that he understood. Blondy smiled, pulled the knife away from the Guard's crotch and slowly let the guard slide down the wall. He then walked over to the kid lying on the floor.

He turned to face the rest of the kids who work working on the production tables, still holding the knife in his hand. The fun he had with the guard hadn't seem to appease the anger he felt inside. He walked along the production tables and stared, or more like glared, at each kid. When he reached the end of the tables, he turned and started back to the other end. Halfway there he stopped, grabbed the young boy who was standing in front of him and put the knife to his throat. A little trickle of blood started to slide down the kid's throat. Blondy looked at the rest of the kids. In Spanish, he told the kids that if anyone of them ever tried to escape, not only would he kill the one who tied to escape, but he would pick someone else at random, and kill them as well. He promised them it would be very painful.

The kid he was holding, with his arm wrapped around his throat, pissed in his pants. As the urine flowed down his leg he froze not knowing what to expect. Nobody breathed. Blondy looked down as the wet spot expanded down the front of the kid's pants and smiled an unbelievably hideous smile. He pushed the kid down on the ground and told him to clean up the mess.

Blondy moved down the line, eyeing each kid as he walked. He then walked over to the kid who was lying on the floor and in one lightning swift move, lifted the kid's head, push the knife blade into the side of his throat and swept it across his windpipe to the other side of his head. The knife went through the kid's throat like a hot knife through butter. It was over in less than two seconds.

The kids and the guards all stared in disbelief and gasped as a pool of blood formed under the partially severed head of the kid. One of the girls passed out and several of them started crying. Even Moustache looked on in stunned silence. He knew Blondy could be brutal, but this was a whole other side. Moustache decided at that point that he needed to be a little more careful around this crazy Gringo.

Blondy looked at the guard who was wiping the blood from his nose and said, "Get this piece of shit out of here and clean this mess up. Make sure no one can find the body." Then he walked off toward the guard's office and closed the door.

Two guards picked up a plastic tarp from under one of the work tables and dumped the body into it. They grabbed two of the girls and told them to get the mess cleaned up. With the body wrapped in plastic, one of the guards went outside and pulled one of the SUVs over to the side door of the warehouse. Looking around carefully to make sure no one was watching they quickly loaded the body into the back of the SUV and closed the

door. Broken Nose then jumped in the SUV
and headed for the gate, which opened
electronically as he approached.

        Broken Nose had never seen anyone
get their head almost cut off. He was
still shaking as he exited the truck
yard. He had to stop for a minute, so at
the end of the street he pulled over to
the side of the road and tried to settle
down. No matter what, he would make sure
no one found the body. He never wanted
to be on the receiving end of one of
Blondy's outbursts.

        Finally, somewhat composed, he
headed east, turned onto 550 and headed
north looking for a good spot to dump the
body. After about twenty miles or so, he
came to a very sharp hairpin turn and
noticed a creek running under the
highway. He pulled onto the shoulder of
the road and turned off the lights. He
sat for a minute. He could see for quite
some ways and since there was no traffic
visible, he climbed out, opened the rear
hatch and pulled out the body.

        He pushed the wrapped body closer
to the edge of the road and started to
unwrap the plastic. His intention was to
slide the body down the slope and let it
drop into the culvert. His mistake was
unwrapping the body so close to the edge
of the road that when he pulled the
plastic away from the body the body went
crashing down into the shrubs below the
culvert. "Shit," was his first thought.

Now what? He tried to climb down into the creek, but the slope was too steep, and he started to slide himself. Pulling back, he thought, "Damn it. No one will find it down there."

He quickly threw the tarp back in the rear, closed the hatch, jumped in the driver's seat and turned the SUV around and headed back to town.

Chapter Twenty Seven

Buck, Terry and the Sheriff stood on the edge of the road near the culvert and watched as the La Plata County Search and Rescue team assisted Dr. Robert Kramer up from the bottom of the culvert. Dr. Kramer is a semi-retired medical doctor and licensed Forensic Pathologist under contract to La Plata County as well as the surrounding counties to perform autopsies. Colorado is one of several states that still operates under the Coroner system instead of the Medical Examiner system. Since the Coroner in La Plata county, Jennifer Bishop, is not a medical doctor, any deaths that require an autopsy, by code, must be performed by a licensed Pathologist. The county hired Dr. Kramer to perform autopsies on an as needed basis.

Dr. Kramer was assisted up the slope, disconnected from the climbing harness and stood to the side as the rescue team pulled up the body, which was wrapped in a black body bag and secured to a rescue sled. The body was then placed in a waiting ambulance to be delivered to the Sheriff's office, where a small autopsy suite along with coolers was set up in the basement. This was a lot more convenient than a few years ago when the bodies had to be taken to Grand Junction for autopsy.

Once Dr. Kramer was comfortable that the body was secure, he signed a transportation order and his pathology assistant entered the ambulance for the ride down the mountain to the Sheriffs' office. The body would be accompanied by his assistant until it was safely locked in one of the four coolers available. This overabundance of caution was needed because the body, especially in a foul play situation, was part of the chain of evidence. The ambulance was followed by a deputy. Just one more precaution against tampering with evidence.

Dr. Kramer walked to his car and removed his Nitrile gloves and his Tyvek one-piece jumpsuit. He rubbed disinfectant on his hands, turned and headed towards the assembled group.

"Sheriff, gentlemen." He said as he approached.

"Dr. Kramer, this is Buck Taylor from CBI and the lead deputy on this case, Terry Rubin." Everyone shook hands and then waited as the Doctor assembled his thoughts.

"Cause of death is pretty obvious," started the Doctor. "His throat was slit pretty much from ear to ear. Deep enough that it was almost severed. Death would have been instantaneous. My experience tells me the assailant had to be a pretty good size guy and was also well trained. The autopsy will reveal more, but my guess is the knife went in just under the right ear and was swiped across the throat to the other side. This is a method that has been refined by the military over the years because the larynx is cut through almost immediately so the victim has no chance to yell out."

Buck interrupted. "So, you're thinking special forces training?"

The Doctor looked at Buck. "First blush. Yes, that would be a good starting point." The Doctor continued. "I will tell you this. That young man suffered one hell of a beating before he was killed. Any one of the blows he suffered could have probably killed him at some point. The knife was final."

Terry asked. "Doctor, were you able to compare the face of the victim to the photo we gave you?" Is it the same guy?"

The Doctor pulled the photo from his shirt pocket and handed it back to Terry. "Hard to tell for sure, not a great picture, but I would say ninety five percent yes."

Everyone stood for a minute, then the Doctor turned to leave.

"Oh. I did take a couple samples from the cuts on his face. We might get some usable DNA from the blood. Gave the samples to Dani. She will bring them up with the rest of the stuff she found. Not much so far. I will start the autopsy as soon as I get back to the office. Sheriff, will one of your guys be attending?"

The Sheriff waved over Quinn and Romero, who were talking with Dani Walker, the forensic tech, who had just climbed up from the culvert. They walked over and stood with the group.

Sheriff said, "The Doc is going to start the autopsy as soon as he gets down the mountain. Would like at least one of you there, can you work that out?'

It was obvious from the reaction of Romero, that he wasn't thrilled with the idea of attending the autopsy, but he waited for his partner to talk. Quinn, who had probably seen quite a few autopsies in his career told the Sheriff that he would head down for the autopsy and that Romero could finish wrapping up the scene. Romero looked relieved. The homicide team walked off towards the cars and Buck figured Quinn was giving Romero last minute instructions for closing out the scene.

The Sheriff looked at Buck and Terry. "For right now I am going to let the homicide team deal with this. Your plates are full. If this turns out to be related to your case, we will decide then what to do."

Buck and Terry both nodded in agreement.

Buck said, "Let's get those blood samples over to the state lab in Pueblo and see if we get any DNA. I will call the lab and let them know it's coming."

Buck checked his watch and realized he had missed lunch, so he hopped in his car and headed down 550 and back into Durango. At College Ave he turned left until he got to East 8th Avenue, turned left and headed up the hill to Fort Lewis College. He knew of an awesome taco truck that usually parked at the campus. It was right where he thought it would be. He ordered two beef tacos and a bottle of Coke and sat down at the park bench opposite the truck. Lunch was gone in a couple gulps and he got back in his car and headed back down the hill.

Chapter Twenty Eight

Buck, the Sheriff and Terry had agreed to meet back in the conference room at the Sheriff's office to go over today's interviews. Buck wanted to stop in and talk to the sneak and peek team and see if they had anything that was usable from the wire taps. Buck headed for his car and just as he sat down his phone rang. It was Hank Clancy, FBI.

"Buck", said Hank. "Have you spoken to Josh or his guys yet today?"

"I was just on my way back to talk to them."

Buck proceeded to tell Hank about the body found in the culvert. He emphasized the fact that the body may not be related to their investigation, but they believed it might be based on the picture from the surveillance team. He told him that the Forensic Pathologist was getting ready to start the autopsy and that they had some blood samples they needed to get to the state crime lab in Pueblo to see if they could get any DNA.

Hank was not pleased that he hadn't been told about the body earlier, but he seemed to get over it pretty quickly.

He said, "OK. Keep me posted. Go see Josh and have him fill you in on the electronics. Also, we did pick up an encrypted sat phone from the NSA satellite survey. The boys in Washington are working on the encryption and once they crack it we will see what's there. They did tell me that the encryption software is top notch, maybe even government or military grade.

Buck told him he would call him in a bit and closed his car door and pulled away. As he did his phone rang again. Jess Gonzales, DEA.

"Buck, it's Jess. Can you talk?"

"Sure Jess, whatcha got?"

"We may have nailed down one of the US enforcers for the Sonoma Cartel. I am sending the info to your phone. This guy is bad news. Name we have on him is Harry Crank. Staff Sergeant. Not sure if that is an alias or real. He spent 6 years in special forces, Green Beret. Dishonorable discharge in 2010 and forty-eight months in a military prison after almost killing four guys in a bar fight. Claimed they jumped him and all he did was defend himself."

According to the Military Police report from Fort Benning, Georgia, Staff Sergeant Crank and two of his trainers were having drinks in a strip joint off base when some guys in the audience started hassling one of the strippers. Somehow, someone got pushed and Sergeant Crank ended up getting a beer spilled on him. According to witnesses, Crank went nuts and started slamming the guys at the other table. By the time he was pulled off by his two buddies, the four college kids at the table looked like they had been through a meat grinder, the bouncers were injured, the dancer had a split lip from getting punched by accident when she tried to run behind the table these guys were sitting at, and they had caused about four grand in damages to the bar.

Everyone who didn't need hospitalization went to jail. The four college kids went to the hospital.   MPs were called and the cops turned over the soldiers to them. Might have been the end of it except Sergeant Crank took exception to being turned over to a black MP and decided to teach him a lesson. Back at the military police jail on base, the MPs removed the cuffs and before anyone could move Sergeant Crank had the black MP in a head lock and almost broke his neck. Took six MPs to separate them.

The result of the bar fight was that of the four kids Crank had put in the hospital, two were released with bandages and casts, one suffered a concussion and a couple broken ribs and one ended up in rehab and will most likely spend the rest of his life in a wheelchair as a quadriplegic. Crank had the book thrown at him. Seems the bar was owned by a state legislator and he knew all four of the kids. Crank got busted down to a private, spent forty-eight months in a military prison and received a dishonorable discharge. Once out, he fell off the grid and hasn't been seen since.

"Why do we think this is one of our guys?" Buck asked.

"Was talking to a couple of our guys who used to work across the border. They said that when the Sonoma Cartel was just getting started there were a lot of violent endings for members of the other cartels. According to rumors, the guy running the ops for the Sonoma Cartel was a tall blond ex Green Beret, who had a real gift for creating violent endings."

She went on to tell him that the guy they heard rumors about was a real whack job. These stories, especially the bad ones, have a way of turning into legends. At some point all the stories, true or not, end up as part of this guy's street cred. Bad part is we don't know what is truth or fiction. We do know that he has travelled between Mexico and the US on several occasions over the years and someone always gets dead. And always in a violent way.

"With this cartel war going on across the border things are changing rapidly, almost daily, and the bodies

keep piling up. If this guy is now
working for the Sonoma Cartel, then
whatever we are dealing with is a big
deal."

"Jess, do we know what this guy did
in special forces?" asked Buck

"Hold on, let me look through his
military record." Buck heard her
clicking keys on her computer. "Holy
shit, Buck. Lot of redacted stuff in his
file. From what I can see, this guy was
one bad ass. Here it is. Last posting
was Benning as a hand-to-hand combat
instructor. Specialty was blade
weapons."

Buck whistled. He told Jess about
the body dump he had just left. Could be
a coincidence that he kid was killed with
a knife in a very military manner. Buck
didn't think so; neither did Jess.

"Buck, if this is one of our guys
in the warehouse, he has about a dozen
outstanding warrants on him. He might be
our way in."

"Jess, is his picture in the stuff
you just sent me?"

"It is," replied Jess.

"Thanks," Buck said. "I will call
you later."

Chapter Twenty Nine

Buck hung up and pulled into the parking lot behind the Sheriff's office.

His first stop was the conference room to talk to the sneak and peek guys. Toby was manning the computers this afternoon and he was listening intently through the headphones that covered both ears. He waved a hand at Buck to acknowledge his presence and pointed to the chair. He then held up one finger, signaling to Buck to wait. He clicked a bunch of computer keys and removed the headphones.

"We are getting some good stuff." He said.

Then he swung the second computer monitor around so Buck could see what he was looking at. On the screen was a live feed from the camera they had placed in the air conditioning duct. Buck put on his reading glasses and leaned in to get a better view of the screen. He was looking at what appeared to be a long assembly line table with a couple dozen

people sitting around the table opening
boxes of toys, removing a piece of the
toy, using a knife to cut a small opening
and then feeding pills of some kind into
the body of the toy. The part that was
removed was then reinstalled, the toy was
replaced in the box and the box was
sealed. It looked like any small factory
in America.

"Can you pan this camera?" Buck
asked.

"Unfortunately, no. This one is
not moveable. "I can zoom in quite a
bit."

The view from the camera began to
grow larger and more defined. Toby took
it to maximum zoom. It gave Buck a
closer view of the people working but not
a great view of the pills. At least not
enough to identify the product. He
watched for a few more minutes and then
leaned back from the screen and scratched
his head.

"Any way we can identify the
pills?" he asked.

Toby shook his head. "I did have a
view last night when someone placed a
huge industrial size pill bottle on the
table. Couldn't read the words on the
bottle so I sent it to Washington to see
if they can do anything with it."

"OK," said Buck. "What else have
you got?"

Toby clicked a few more keys and the screen changed to a view of a computer worksheet. He proceeded to explain to Buck that they were able to isolate one computer from the work space and three computers from the office area. The ones from the office didn't give any indication of what was going on in the warehouse. The analysts worked all night on the computers and from what they could tell, it was almost like two different businesses were being run out of the space. The books for the trucking company were clean. No odd write-offs, no mysterious entries. Just a very simple accounting program. All the billing receipts match up with deliveries and all the manifests looked normal. The analysts even compared past invoicing to the invoicing for the past couple weeks and nothing had changed.

The other computer is another story. We gave access to the NSA and they are still having trouble getting in. The encryption is first rate and very high end. They think they are making progress. The NSA was able to crack the encryption on the one sat phone they locked on. According to Toby, there was only one call made today and it sounded like a very simple report. All is good, on schedule, that kind of thing. Nothing was said that was definitive about a shipping date.

Buck sat back. He was hoping for more. He was almost disappointed. Then

Toby dropped the bomb. Since the building's electrical system was being used as a gigantic voice tap, it can pick up even the quietist conversation. Basically, no place to hide. It seems that one of the guards must have gotten beat up by the boss and the guard was still pissed off that he had been disrespected. He told the guy he was talking to that he would get even with the boss as soon as they got this first shipment out of the way. He would settle the score. Toby reminded Buck that this conversation had taken place in Spanish. He offered to play it for Buck, but Buck's Spanish was rudimentary at best.

He shook his head and Toby continued the debrief. The guard, it seems, was really pissed at himself for letting that kid almost escape, but that did not give the boss cause to punch him in front of all those kids. The boss had disrespected him and to make matters worse, he made him dump the body. The guard sounded like he had a strong connection to the big boss and would make the other boss pay. His pal reminded him that the Gringo boss was crazy. That he slit that kid's throat without even thinking about it. At that point someone else walked into the room and told them their break was over and get back to work.

Buck pushed forward in his chair. He looked at Toby with a surprised look on his face. Almost to stunned to talk.

"Is that what they actually said?
That the Gringo boss slit the kid's
throat?"

Toby nodded. "That's how we
translated it. Does this mean
something?"

Buck replied. 'We found a body
dumped off the highway north of town
today. Young Mexican kid with his throat
slit. Can't be a coincidence."

Toby replied. "Holy shit. But does
this give us enough to go after him.
Right now, all we have is two guys
talking."

Buck thought for a minute. "At
this point we don't even know who this
guy is. We have some info from the DEA
on a possible guy but no proof he is even
here. If it is the same guy and we can
prove he is here it might help our cause
and give us a way in. It might not get
us a warrant on its own but with
everything else we have it might be
enough. Let's see what the Sheriff
thinks."

Toby said, "You think this kid was
killed in front of the others as a
lesson?"

Buck thought for a minute. "Yeah.
That would be my read. Anything else?"

Toby nodded. "Just typical work
environment chatter. These kids are
being abused by the guards, but they

don't say much. I think they are just plain scared. Last night after we activated the voice taps, we picked up some crying coming from somewhere in the space. Possibly from the cages we spotted when we set the camera. The guards make small talk, but nothing about what's going on."

Toby looked unsure about the next part of the debrief. Buck looked at him.

"You got something else?" Buck asked.

"Not sure what it means but I think one of the bosses is having sex with some of the young girls. We picked up some, what I guess you could call, grunts and some screams. The whole lead up to the grunts made it sound like the girl did not want to go and she kept pleading with someone else to stop it. The second voice, sounded American, definite Sothern accent. He just laughed. The sex sounded pretty rough."

Buck looked at Toby. "OK. Keep listening. Can you copy the conversation about the body to a disc, so the Sheriff can get it to the District Attorney?"

Toby said he could and Buck told him that they had done good, but to keep working on the computer.

Buck got up and headed towards the Sheriff's office. If this is the same guy Jess had sent him the info on then they could possibly go after him on one

of the outstanding warrants. They needed
to prove it is the same guy.

     Buck hated this point in an
investigation. Things were starting to
open up but they were still missing a lot
of pieces. He thought back on the
picture of the kids working at the table.
How had they been able to sneak that many
people, as a group, into the US without
someone noticing? He wanted to dismiss
the first thought he had but it sat there
nagging at his brain. These guys had
help getting across the border and they
were getting help bringing in huge
quantities of pills, probably Oxy, but
from where? He knew anything
manufactured in the US was carefully
controlled. But if not from here, then
where? After all, the papers were full
of stories about the huge rise in opioid
addictions. The President had just
recently declared it a National Medical
Emergency. This was serious stuff, yet
from looking at the pictures and the
number of trailers sitting in the
trucking company yard, they were bringing
this stuff in without any trouble.

Chapter Thirty

Buck stopped off in his temporary office, sat down at his desk, pulled out his phone and dialed the number for Max Clinton. Dr. Maxine Clinton was a matronly woman in her early sixties, about five feet five with short grey hair. She probably thought she carried around an extra fifteen pounds she didn't need but she was still a handsome woman. Married for 40 years, Max had 4 children, eleven grandchildren and 6 great grandchildren. She lived in a 150-year-old farm house in Pueblo, where she liked to tend her garden and sit on her porch and drink iced tea. She was also a bourbon girl and could easily drink most people under the table. She was loud and outspoken, but she knew her job.

Max received her PhD in Biology from the University of Colorado and had worked as a biology professor for 20 years before joining CBI. Currently, she was head of the state crime lab, a job she thoroughly enjoyed. She was a tough task master, but she had a belief system

that didn't allow for defeat. Her goal
was to give the crime investigator, no
matter which department or municipality
they worked for, all the information they
would need to solve any crime. She held
that as a sacred obligation to the
victims. She was incredibly dedicated
and her team at the lab practically
worshipped her.

Buck would have been included in
that group. Many times, during a tough
investigation, it was Max and her team
that lit the spark that led to a break
through. Max was one of Buck's favorite
people and she felt the same way about
him.

Maxine answered her phone on the
fourth ring. "Hey Buck. How's my
favorite cop?"

"Doing great", Buck replied.

"I bet not if your calling old Max.
What can I do to make your day?"

"I have some blood samples heading
your way from Durango. I need to see if
we can get DNA from the samples for
anyone other than the victim. It's a
pretty crucial ask"

Max asked. "Is this for the
possible cartel thing? The Director
already called me and told me to put
everything on the back burner if you
called. He didn't go into details but
said this was top priority. He even
authorized us to spend the money for an

overnight DNA test. Those are not cheap, and he told me it didn't matter. God, Buck, what have you gotten yourself into now?"

Buck filled Max in on some of the details about the case and what they had to date. When he spoke the words out loud, it really didn't seem like they had much of a case. But then when he thought about the fact that he had only arrive yesterday morning, maybe things weren't so bleak.

Max agreed. Max was always good for his ego. She seemed to always know just the right words to say to keep his head on straight. She always said, if she could deal with her huge family, she could deal with pretty much anything. She had proven that time and again and Buck was always grateful for her insights. She may not have been a cop, but she knew more about crime than anyone he knew. She listened carefully as Buck spoke. Not interrupting until he was finished giving her the high points.

"You know Buck. It sounds to me like you guys are pretty much one break away from closing this thing down. It will either come from the science or it will come from the electronics, you just watch. In the meantime, I will get the blood samples going as soon as we have them in our hot little hands."

Buck thanked her, and she ended the conversation the way she always did.

"God will watch over you Buck Taylor.
You are a good man. Stay safe."

     Buck wasn't much of a religious
man. He hadn't been to church in
probably forty years. He had been raised
Catholic but left the church right after
Confirmation. He always had too many
questions about the teachings and too
many people telling him that he had to
have faith. That wasn't the answer he
was looking for. He had a lot of
friends, Max among them, who always
offered up a prayer and especially when
Lucy was dying. He never once rejected
any of those offers. Often smiling and
thanking them for their kind thoughts.

     Buck had realized a long time ago
that it wasn't God and faith that he had
a problem with, it was organized
religion. In his many years in law
enforcement he had seen too many times
the after effects of someone's religious
beliefs. It amazed him that so many
people of faith could cause so much
hatred and crime. But then non-believers
created just as much havoc.

     Buck always believed there was
probably a higher power out there but he
didn't believe that whatever that power
was that it really cared about one
individual over another. His football
coach always offered up a prayer before
each game asking for help in defeating
the other team. He always suspected the
other team's coach probably was doing the

same thing. How did God decide which team should win?

He knew a lot of people who said a lot of prayers for Lucy over the five years she was sick, but in the end, she still died. And she was the last person who should have gotten cancer. But Buck didn't carry any hatred. Who could he possibly get mad at? Who could he blame?

Buck believed that there were spirits or a force all around us and he always thanked them for allowing him to enjoy the hike, or for allowing him to catch fish, or see the sunrise and the sunset. It wasn't religion. It was something deeper. Something Buck really didn't understand. He just accepted it. But no matter what, he always appreciated it when Max told him that God was watching over him. After all. What could it hurt?

Buck hung up his phone and sat back in his chair. He picked up his phone and dialed Jess Gonzales, DEA.

Jess answered. "Hey Buck, what's up?" He filled her in on the electronics results so far. She listened intently.

"Sounds like this could be the same guy. We just need to prove he is actually in the warehouse."

"Yeah," replied Buck. "Easier said than done. But that wasn't all I called for. If we are dealing with huge

quantities of oxy, where is the stuff
coming from?"

She thought for a minute and said.
"Great question. We have been wondering
the same thing since this all came to
light. We have tight controls on
everything manufactured in the US and
Canada, so we are certain it is not
coming from inside the US, especially
with the possible quantities involved.
Some of my guys are wondering if it is
coming from someplace way off, like China
or Pakistan or somewhere else out there.
Probably getting shipped into Mexico. At
this point we don't have a solid answer."

Buck replied, "OK, let's say it is
from overseas. How is it getting across
the border?"

Jess was a little hesitant. "We
have some thoughts but I am going to keep
those in house for a while yet. We may
have a better idea once this is over."

"You think the cartel is getting
help on our side, don't you?"

"Look Buck. Let's wrap this up
first. Anything else is federal and we
will deal with it. Sorry I can't be more
specific."

"No problem Jess. I gotta run.
Let's talk later."

Buck hung up the phone. He sensed
Jess knew more than she was saying. He
understood that whatever she knew was

federal and he was just a local cop, but he also respected the fact that she had a much bigger job to do than he had, and he was grateful for the help.

Buck got up from his desk, walked down the hall to the kitchen and grabbed another Coke out of the refrigerator. He opened it, took a big gulp and looked out the window. How did we get here, he thought as he looked out over the sleepy little town? How could something so ugly show up in a place so beautiful? Buck knew one thing for certain. Evil might have arrived here but he would make sure it didn't stay and that it didn't go anywhere else. This was the world he lived in and he wasn't going to let anything ruin it.

Buck left the kitchen and went in search of the Sheriff and Terry Rubin.

Chapter Thirty One

Blondy was sitting in the little guard's office in the warehouse talking on the encrypted sat phone. The conversation was in Spanish. Moustache was sitting on the other side of the desk. He had spent the last 15 minutes filling in the Boss about progress and about the kid he had to make an example of. He knew the Boss would approve. The Boss would have done the same thing and it would most likely have been a lot more brutal. In the two years since he started working for the Sonoma Cartel, he had seen and done a lot of horrific things but the things he had witnessed the Boss do were so much worse.

When Carlos Rojas wanted something, he didn't care who got in his way, men, women, old people, kids. It didn't matter. Carlos would have probably cut off his own mother's head if it got him what he wanted. Brutal was an understatement when it came to Rojas and the more brutal the better.

Blondy stopped talking and listened. He said. "No problem, sir. We can make that happen."

Blondy hung up the phone, looked at Moustache and said, "The Boss wants to move up the timetable. Instead of shipping out the first loads on Tuesday, he wants to do it Sunday morning. He has already alerted our other locations to expect the shipments and be ready to re-ship within a couple days. What do you think? Can we be ready?"

Moustache thought for a moment and said, "That only gives us two days. We still have one and a half trailers to load. We should be OK. We will need to push these kids to get done. It would be better if we had that kid you sliced. He was a hard worker."

Blondy smiled. "Yeah, well that's too damn bad. We needed to make an example of the kid. Water under the bridge."

"Ok. You're the boss. I will start pushing the kids. No sleep tonight."

Moustache stood up to leave. Blondy said, "Sit a minute. Couple other things. I told the Boss that I am getting a twitchy feeling in the back of my brain. Not sure what's going on, but when I get the twitch I always pay attention. Make sure the guards keep their eyes open. Second. He's concerned that Dick and Hector might not be fully onboard. We may have to handle them."

Moustache interrupted. "This is a small town man. Somebody gonna notice one of those guys goes missing. Maybe we can increase the money each month, see if they come around."

Blondy thought for a minute. "OK. Offer them another hundred K each and let's see if that makes them more cooperative. Last thing. When we are done here the Boss wants his nephew to take over running the operation and he wants us back home. He is having some problems and he needs us to deal with them. He wants his nephew to run a minimum of four trucks a week out of here and he is thinking about bringing up the first load of liquid cocaine and meth. He wants this place fully operational by the end of the month'.

Moustache looked at him. "OK, but you and I both know that kid is an idiot. He let that kid almost get over the fence. You also better hope he didn't somehow get word to his uncle that you punched him in front of everybody. These wackos have pride and you twisted his up a bunch. You sure we ain't going home to get slaughtered?"

Blondy got a serious look on his face. "Don't know for sure."

"Look man. We got us a boat load
of money. Maybe it's time to move on.
Maybe Europe or someplace like that."

"Knock that shit off. You know the
Boss could find us anywhere. We're in
this for the long haul. Besides, if we
bailed, Rojas would not stop looking for
us until we were dead. I don't want to
spend the rest of my life looking over my
shoulder."

Moustache nodded, got up from the
chair and headed into the warehouse.
Blondy sat and thought for a minute. He
hadn't considered when he punched the
Boss's nephew, that he was stepping over
a family line. He was maintaining
discipline. He hoped that this time his
temper hadn't gotten him in trouble.
Blondy opened the screen on the encrypted
laptop, pulled up a contact list and sent
out a group email to his drivers letting
them know to be at the warehouse at four
AM Sunday morning. He wondered why the
Boss moved up the time table, but then
what did it matter? He needed to be
ready no matter what.

Moustache walked along the
production line and started yelling in
Spanish that they had to get the last
truck loaded by the end of the day
tomorrow. No one would be sleeping
tonight. The kids never flinched. They
just kept their heads down and kept
working. He then headed over to the
guard that Blondy had punched and pulled

him towards the loading dock door and out of earshot of the office.

"Your uncle is going to leave you here to run this operation after we are done." He said to the guard. "Your uncle wants us back in Mexico after the loads go out. Did you somehow get word to your uncle about getting punched?"

The guard looked at him with surprise. He was ready to deny anything. He didn't trust Moustache and thought this might be a test or something. He answered in Spanish, "hell no, man. You know me better than that. Rojas would kill him if he found out."

Moustache knew he was lying. Pride was a big factor in the cartel world, as was family, until it wasn't. He wasn't sure how the nephew had gotten the word back to Rojas, but it was obvious that he had. Moustache smiled.

"Maybe you should say something." He walked away.

The guard wasn't sure what just happened, but he was starting to get the idea that maybe things weren't all that rosy between Blondy and Moustache and that Moustache was covering his bets. Something to think about.

Chapter Thirty Two

Claire cringed whenever the door between the old warehouse and the other warehouse, as she referred to it, opened. Blondy made her nervous but when it was Moustache who came into the office she felt almost dirty. It was probably the way he stood in front of her desk and leered at her. No one had ever looked at her like that and it made her feel cheap and used.

The door to the other warehouse opened and in walked Moustache. He stopped at her desk and with that lecherous smile asked her how her day was going. Trying to be polite, the way she had been raised, she told him her day was fine. He told her he could make her nights fine too and then he laughed a disgusting laugh and headed back towards the offices. After each encounter with him she wondered to herself, how was she ever going to be able to stay in this job if he was part of the package. She felt like she needed a shower.

Moustache found Hector siting at his desk working on the computer. Hector smiled and invited him to have a seat, which Moustache did. Moustache was thinking that Hector was coming around to having them as part of his business. He felt that Hector was beginning to like the money, even though he had only received one payment so far, but he seemed to be adapting better than Dick was.

Hector was starting to enjoy the money. He was very careful how he spent it and he hadn't yet told his wife about the off-shore account, but he was able to take her to dinner a couple times and to buy her a pretty bracelet for no reason at all. His wife felt it was extravagant but she didn't force him to return it and she wore it every day.

Hector stopped clicking computer keys and looked at Moustache.

"Everything OK?" He asked.

"Where is your partner?" Moustache asked.

"He is meeting with a prospective client. Can I do anything for you or do you need to see him?"

Moustache liked the fact that they were still chasing business. It made him feel more like they were getting the hang of working for the cartel and were trying to keep their piece of the business working.

"The Boss thinks you might not be comfortable with our arrangement. Is that true?" Moustache asked.

"No," replied Hector. "We are fine. Dick had a little trouble coming around but he seems OK now. We have tried to stay out of your way just as we were told to do."

"That is good, because we wouldn't want you to be unhappy. Unhappy people cause problems." Moustache smiled.

"Did we do something wrong?" asked Hector looking very nervous.

Moustache told him that the Boss liked to have happy employees and partners and so towards that end he was going to give them each an additional fifty K each month. Just so they would feel appreciated. He wasn't sure why he lied about the amount that him and Blondy had agreed on. Maybe he was starting to think too much. Him and Blondy had known each other a long time and they trusted each other. Or did they. Hector smiled, said thank you and was there anything else he could help him with.

"Just make sure your partner appreciates our generosity."

Moustache stood up and walked out the office door. Hector was relieved that there was no problem and pleased with what he had just heard. A couple months of this and we might be able to get out of this little town he thought,

and go someplace far away. Now he had to
make sure Dick went along. He would hate
to see something terrible happen to Dick.

        Hector told Dick about the
increased monthly payment when he got
back to the office. Dick was not
pleased. He had been quiet for the last
couple weeks about this new arrangement
but he hadn't accepted this whole thing
yet. It also bothered him that Hector
seemed to be going along quite willingly.

        Dick walked out of Hector's office,
sat down at his own desk, put his hands
up to his head and pushed his hair back.
He was concerned that once whatever was
going on next door was finished that
either he or Hector would be expendable.
He knew that the work next door wasn't a
onetime thing and that he would have to
keep up a false face from now on. He was
also concerned that he could end up in
prison and that scared him to death.

Chapter Thirty Three

Buck found the Sheriff in her office. She was talking on her desk phone and pointed to the chair opposite her desk. Buck sat down. The chair was an old padded black leather chair and although it had seen better days it was still comfortable. Buck sat back and waited for the Sheriff to finish her conversation. The Sheriff clicked off.

"Hell of a day." She said. "I am glad we don't have many days like the last couple. People are running a little ragged. By the way. That was Dr. Kramer. He was calling with the preliminary autopsy results. Just as we figured. The kid died from massive blood loss caused by the slice through his neck. Nothing unusual there. The Doc did say that the facial contusions and the body bruises were recent, probably within a couple hours of his death. One thing he noticed that was a little strange, was a lot of earlier bruising. Doc figures this kid has been getting beaten for months. Some of the old bruises were almost too faded to see."

Buck thought about that for a minute.

"I'm guessing," he said "This is probably how they keep these kids in line. Beatings, drugs, you name it. Any early tox info?"

"No tox screen yet. Too early. He did take a few more swabs and he pulled some material out from under his nails. Who knows? Maybe the killer left us some DNA. He packaged up the clothes and the new swabs and along with the earlier blood swabs he sent it all to the state crime lab, by courier service. The lab should get it later tonight or first thing in the morning."

"Detective Quinn is finishing up with the Doc and will be up in a bit to write it all up. At least right now there is nothing that points to any connection between the murder and the warehouse except for the electronics, which right now is uncorroborated."

Buck said, "Maybe after we get the labs back. Let's wait and see. In the meantime, I think we should take a run at the two guys who own the trucking company. Maybe we can get something from one of them."

"You think that's wise?" asked the Sheriff. "We don't know how deep these guys are in. Might tip our hand."

"Yeah. Been thinking about that.
I know this guy Dick has been crying in
his beer and now with Claire on the run,
maybe Dick is our in. Let's wait til our
guys pick up Claire and get a chance to
talk to her. Might give us some new
insight into which way to go. They
should be picking her up right about
now."

"OK." Said the Sheriff. "The local
newspaper hound keeps calling the desk
wanting to know about a possible dead
body. That's gonna be a big story around
here. How do you think we should play
it?"

"Can we hold him off for a little
while until we know if it is connected or
not. Somebody tried to hide the body,
and as of right now, they probably don't
know we found it. I'd like to keep it
that way."

"Got it. Let me see what I can do
to keep stalling him."

"Where you headed?" she asked.

"I was gonna grab some food and
head back to the hotel. Need to fill out
a report for the Director on progress so
far. Gonna be a short report. Call if
you need me."

Buck got out of the comfortable
chair, walked out the door to the
Sheriff's office and headed for his car.
He was just opening the door that led to

the parking lot when Terry Rubin pushed
it open.

"Hey Buck. I was looking for you."

"Well" replied Buck. "Here I am.
What's up?"

Terry was concerned with the lack
of progress they had been making. Buck
liked this young fella. He had a lot of
drive. He also wasn't as young as Buck
thought. Buck figured when he met Terry,
yesterday that he was in his late
twenties, early thirties. He couldn't
have been more wrong. Terry was actually
forty-six. He had received a Bachelor's
degree in Criminology from University of
Colorado in Boulder and had graduated
from the FBI Forensics Academy, which the
FBI ran each year to teach local law
enforcement officers how to run an
investigation and gather evidence. It
was a highly sought after program and the
FBI prided themselves on only taking the
best the states had to offer. On some
occasions, the FBI made job offers to the
top ranked students in the class. Terry
had been offered a job but had turned it
down due to his family situation.

He spent ten years with the Salt
Lake City Police Department before
transferring to La Plata County. He had
been with the Sheriff's Office for nearly
ten years. At first, he wasn't thrilled
with the pace of life in Durango, but he
had no choice. His wife's mom was
ailing, and his wife wanted to be close.

Even though his mother in law had passed away five years ago Terry had gotten comfortable in his new surroundings and his family had set down roots. With his young looks he was a perfect fit for undercover drug work, considering Durango was a college town, and he thrived in his new job.

Terry followed Buck to his car.

"What do you think if we go after either Dick or Hector? Maybe we can shake something loose."

Buck smiled. "Sheriff and I were just talking about that very thing. We are going to wait until the CBI team talks to Claire Ringsby and see if she might be able to give us some insight into which one might be best. Good thought though."

"Great minds." Said Terry. "You gonna call it a night?"

"Yeah. Why don't you wrap up for today and we can pick up fresh in the morning?"

Terry said that he had some paperwork to do to and he would close up in a little while. He wished Buck a good night and headed back to the side door of the Sheriff's Department. Buck got in his car and sat for a minute trying to decide what he wanted to eat. What he really wanted was a good steak, so he headed out to 550, turned north and headed for Charlie's Roadhouse, a little steak place just out past the northern edge of Durango.

Buck loved Charlie's and tried to get there at least once anytime he was in the area. It was a unique little place. From the outside it looked like an old log cabin. Inside it had an old west charm. Dark wood, worn red vinyl cushions but it was the menu that was unique. They offered four different cuts of steak: ribeye, NY, filet and sirloin. They recently started offering a chicken dish. The steak came with a baked potato and vegetable. You could get a salad, but they only had ranch dressing. That was the entire menu. Buck didn't know where they got their meat from but he had never tasted meat so tender in his life. He liked the simplicity of the place and he was never disappointed with the meal.

Buck finished the last little bit of the ribeye he was eating and the waitress came by and refilled his glass of Coke. She took his plate and he sat back to just enjoy the moment. He tried to focus for a minute on the case but with all the background noise in the restaurant it was hard to concentrate. He finished his Coke, paid the check the waitress had left on the corner of the table for him and stepped out into the night air. The last couple days had been hot but the nights were almost perfect. In the mountains the air cools off fast as the sun is going down but in the summer it never gets too cold. Just

comfortable. The sun was starting to
cast long shadows across the parking lot.
Buck headed for his hotel.

Chapter Thirty Four

Terry Rubin was just wrapping up his reports and was getting ready to head home. Tonight, was spaghetti night and his wife Maria, who was of Italian descent, made some of the best meatballs Terry had ever tasted. He always thought it was her cooking that attracted him to her when they were first dating. Her parents had owned an Italian restaurant in Salt Lake City and it was obvious that she had learned to cook from the best.

Deep in thought about meatballs and fried mozzarella sticks, Terry snapped out of it as he walked past the conference room. Randall was sitting at the table with Josh and they were very rapidly typing on their laptops. Josh saw Terry standing in the hallway and waved for him to come in. Terry stepped into the conference room and walked over to the table. He was watching the computer screens on both laptops and was amazed at how fast Randall was typing away on the keyboard. The screens stopped moving and they all read what was on the screen in front of them.

Terry looked at the two men. "Is this for real?" he asked.

Josh nodded. "We just confirmed it with NSA. They picked up the whole conversation on the encrypted sat phone. We only had one side."

Terry looked confused. "Can you explain this to me so I understand what you have?"

Randall took over. "You bet. We picked up a conversation between two people. They were talking quietly, but like we said, the whole space is one big voice tap so we get everything nice and clear. Just prior to these guys talking, one of the guys was talking on the sat phone. Even though it was in Spanish the guy definitely had a southern accent. Anyway, after we heard the conversation between the two guys on site we hooked up with the NSA to confirm what we heard and to see what was being said on the other end of the phone, since they get both sides of the conversation. They just sent us the translation transcript and we were confirming it with our translation from the site."

"OK," replied Terry. "Whatcha got?"

"The local guy must have been talking to the big boss. He told the boss about making an example of one of

the kids who tried to escape and that he
had to slit his throat. The boss seemed
pleased but also concerned. He wants to
move up the shipping date to Sunday
morning."

Terry almost couldn't breathe. "He
actually said he had to slit a kid's
throat?"

"Yeah," replied Josh. "And he told
the guy on the other end of the phone
that he had the guard dispose of the body
in the mountains."

"Holy shit. If we can figure out
which one did it, we got them. Nice
work. Now what about this shipping date
thing?"

Randall took over. "Sounds like
they were originally going to ship on
Tuesday, but the big boss is edgy and
wants to go Sunday morning. They just
sent out a blast text to what is probably
their drivers to be at the warehouse at
four AM Sunday morning."

Terry was almost giddy. "Awesome.
Now we have a date and time. We have
been waiting for this kind of break."
Terry was pulling out his phone when Josh
stopped him.

"Hold on cowboy. There's more.
The southern accent guy is getting
twitchy. Told the other guy he is
getting this itch in the back of his neck
that somethings up and he always pays
attention to the itch. It might be

because he punched the guard who let the kid try to escape and it turns out the guard is the big boss's nephew and he is supposed to be running things once this shipment leaves. The two guys talking are being recalled to Mexico. One guy questioned if it might be to get slaughtered for punching the nephew. They talked about running, but southern accent guy shut him down. Now here is the good part. A few minutes later, heavy Mexican accent asked another guy, we are thinking the nephew, if he had reported the punch and the disrespect to his uncle. The guard denied doing it, but heavy accent suggested maybe he should. Not sure what that was all about."

Terry sat down in one of the chairs at the conference table and thought about this development. The two guys who seem to be running things have been recalled by the big boss. They don't know if the guard he punched, the nephew, told the uncle anything but there is some concern that being recalled to Mexico might mean payback for the disrespect. Then the one guy talks to the nephew and practically tells him to tell his uncle about the punch. Randall suggested it sounds like heavy accent is trying to protect his ass and maybe even get the other guy killed. Everybody kind of nodded in agreement.

"Have you called Buck?" Terry asked.

"Not yet. You got it first."
Replied Josh.

"OK. Can you put this all together
and send it out to the whole team, your
boss, DEA and CBI and I will call Buck?
He went to dinner, so I am going to go
home, grab a bite and then call him.
Give him a chance to digest his food.
Nice job, guys."

Terry headed for the door, hopped
in his car and headed home for a quick
dinner. Things were coming together.

Chapter Thirty Five

Buck pulled into the parking lot of his hotel, turned off the car, opened his door, got out and walked around to the rear hatch to grab his backpack. He opened the backpack to make sure his laptop was inside and zipped it back up. He wanted to spend time tonight going over the file that Jess Gonzales, DEA, had emailed him about Harry Crank. He felt that what she had read to him over the phone earlier was a possible match for the guy who killed the Mexican kid, but he wanted to really sit down and digest the file. Buck always believed the devil was in the details in any investigation. He felt the file on this guy was a good break.

He slung one of the straps of his backpack over his right shoulder and started walking towards the door to the hotel. Just as Buck was passing the last row of cars, the door to the hotel opened and out stepped a tall rangy looking blond guy. He had a physique that told Buck he was in excellent condition. All sinew and muscles. His hair was not too long and was what you might call scraggly. What stopped Buck in his tracks was the tattoo he saw on his right arm, visible just below the sleeve of his green T-shirt. The tattoo showed a skull with a dagger through it. Definitely Green Beret.

Buck had seen those tattoos way too many times while he was an MP during his time in the army. Buck's mind was trying to grasp what he was looking at when he heard a voice on his left side calling his name. Buck turned his head to the left just in time to see Jess Gonzales coming out from between two cars and waving at him. At the very same moment he heard a voice from his right yell out "Hey Cop." Buck looked to his right and saw two guys coming from either side of the row of parked cars. Each guy had on a baseball cap and was carrying a semi-automatic pistol.

Now Buck had never really dealt with metaphysical stuff and he didn't believe in coincidence, but when he would look back on this entire incident it was like some weird cosmic convergence. Here was Buck, here was the possible Green Beret bad guy, here was Jess Gonzales and here were two guys with guns. It seemed to Buck that at that moment everything went into slow motion.

Buck threw his backpack off his right shoulder, flipped the thumb break on his holster and grabbed his gun. Somewhere behind him, someone yelled "GUN!!" The Green Beret looked first towards Buck and then towards the two guys with guns, not sure what to do. He started moving to his right away from where this was all taking place as the two guys with the guns raised them up into firing position and started pulling the triggers as they were closing the gap. Three other people, coming out the front door of the hotel, stopped for a moment and then dove back inside the hotel.

Buck, using his peripheral vision while keeping an eye on the two shooters, looked for cover. Not seeing any, he dropped to a crouch just as the first bullet flew over his head, pretty much where his chest had been just a nanosecond before. Now instinct and training kicked in as Buck drew his pistol firing just as the weapon cleared his holster. Then firing twice more as he brought the gun up to his shooting position. Two of his rounds found their mark and he could see a big splash of red blossom across the chest of the shooter on the right. More bullets flew past him as he turned his sights on the other shooter. At that instant he could hear a volley of explosions from behind him and the other shooter's gun flew up in the air and he smashed into the car behind him, slid down the door and sat there not moving. Buck spun around with his gun up and quickly saw Jess Gonzales standing about fifteen feet away, leaning over the hood of a car with her gun positioned in front of her.

Buck swung back around, keeping his gun aimed at the two shooters lying on the ground.

"You OK?" he yelled.

"Good." Came the reply from Jess who was now running across the rest of the drive aisle with her gun pointed at the shooters.

Buck had moved in on the guy he had taken down and kicked the gun out of the way. Looking back to make sure Jess was nearby, he bent over and touched two fingers to the neck of shooter number one. It was obvious from the amount of blood on the ground around him that the shooter was dead, but Buck checked for a pulse anyway.

Jess was standing about five feet behind him watching him while also keeping an eye on shooter number two. As Buck stood back up, she moved to the shooter now propped up against the car door and checked his pulse. Buck was now covering her with his gun. She looked up at Buck and shook her head. Shooter two was also gone.

She holstered her weapon and walked towards Buck. Sirens, lots of them, could be heard in the distance coming from all directions. Buck holstered his gun. His hands were shaking. The two dead shooters didn't bother Buck. He had been involved in several shootouts during his long career. A lot of cops go through their entire careers never using their weapon. In his career, Buck had used his weapon three times and each time a bad guy had died. No, it wasn't the dead shooters that bothered him, it was how close that one bullet had come to ending his life.

Jess's face was ashen. This was the first time in her career that she had killed a man. She had been in shootouts before, but never one on one. She steadied herself and looked at Buck.

"What the hell, Buck?" She asked. "Who the hell are these guys?"

"No idea."

Buck knelt back down next to shooter number one and pushed his baseball cap off his head. He stood up, walked over to shooter two and did the same thing. His mind was clearing and then the realization set in.

"The Slattery brothers." He said.

"Who the hell are the Slattery brothers and why did they just try to off you?" She replied. "Are these guys part of what we are working on?"

Buck shook his head. "No. Case I was working in Teller county. Triple

homicide. We were waiting on DNA before
we arrested these guys. Prime suspects."

Three Durango Police Department
cars rolled into the parking lot with
lights flashing and sirens wailing. The
cops stopped about twenty feet away and
exited the cars with guns drawn. Buck
held up both hands, as did Jess, to let
them know there was no threat and in his
right hand was his badge, which he had
removed from his belt.

"Cops, on the job." He yelled.

Still cautious, the first officer
to his left approached Buck and Jess.
The two other cops held their positions
and covered their man. Buck told the
officer that he was going to reach slowly
into his back right pocket and pull out
his ID. Gun still trained on Buck, the
officer said, "slowly."

Buck removed his ID and handed it
very slowly to the cop, who took it with
his left hand and opened it up. Looking
at the picture and then looking at Buck,
he closed the wallet, handed it back. He
then looked at Jess and asked her to take
out her ID, also slowly, and hand it to
him. Jess complied and he went through
the same exercise. Convinced the
situation was under control, he handed
Jess back her ID and holstered his
weapon. His fellow officers did the same
and then moved up to see what had
transpired. The first officer clicked
the microphone he had hooked to the

collar of his shirt and called for an
ambulance and a supervisor. He reported
the shooting and that there were law
enforcement personnel involved and gave
the all clear.

        By this time two more Durango
police cars had entered the lot and the
officers were starting to put up
barricades at the driveway entrances so
no one could leave or enter. At almost
the same time, two Sheriff's department
cars arrived and a black civilian car.
One of the marked cars contained Sheriff
Sinclair who got out and walked over to
Buck and Jess. Terry Rubin badged his
way past the cops putting up the
barricades. They all stood around
looking at the two dead shooters.

Chapter Thirty Six

The ambulance was cleared into the parking lot followed by another Durango Police Department marked unit. This one contained Chief of Police Gilbert Chandler. Gil was a solid built man of forty five, with slightly graying hair. He stood about five ten and weighed about one sixty five. He had been the Chief of Police in Durango for the past ten years. He was well respected in the community. He immediately took charge. The Chief and Buck went way back and he knew Jess from a DEA raid that his department had been a part of a couple years back. He shook hands and looked at the two shooters on the ground.

"Well Buck. You sure know how to keep things interesting. Any idea who these two are?" He pointed at the bodies.

"Yeah. The Slattery brothers. This one is Mike and that one is Todd." Buck pointed towards each body.

"They part of what you guys are working on?" the Chief asked. He had been apprised of the current investigation by Sheriff Sinclair. He had offered her his help as needed.

"No" replied Buck. "These two are, were, prime suspects in a triple homicide in Teller County I was working on before I got the call to come here. We were stalled in the investigation and waiting on DNA results."

"Any idea how they tracked you here?" asked the Sheriff.

"No idea at all. Teller County was supposed to be sitting on these two until we were ready to make an arrest. Might have overheard something while we had them in for questioning. Not sure."

The Chief looked at Jess. "And what's your story young lady?"

Jess replied. "I had just gotten here so I could talk to Buck about the investigation. I saw Buck at just about the same time these two showed themselves and then all hell broke loose."

"Sounds like you were in the right place at the right time, Jess." replied the Chief. Jess just stood there with her arms wrapped across her chest.

The Chief next directed one of the police officers two get two evidence bags and asked Buck and Jess to hand over their weapons. They both pulled the magazines, racked the slides to dump the next round out of the chambers and handed the weapons and the mags to the officer, who placed them in the bags, noted the date and time on the bags, sealed the bags and signed his name on the flaps. He handed the bags to the Chief.

The Chief then pulled out his phone and called Dr. Kramer, the Forensic Pathologist, and asked him to hurry over to the hotel. That done and while he had his phone out, he snapped several pictures of the bodies insitu, as they lie. He directed his officers to cordon off the area around the bodies and asked everyone in the area to step outside the police tape. Since this was not related to the drug investigation, he asked the Sheriff if her homicide detectives could handle the interviews and he directed two of his officers to go into the hotel lobby and see if they could get the names and contact info for anyone who had seen the incident. He told them to get preliminary witness statements.   The Chief asked Jess and Buck to head over to the Durango Police Headquarters. He put them in separate patrol cars.

The Sheriff called Quinn, filled him in and asked him to grab Dani Walker, her Forensic Tech, and head over. They would be handling the investigation. She told him to send Romero over to Police Headquarters and start the interviews. She had been filled in by Josh about the new timeline at the trucking company and she wanted this shooting investigation wrapped up ASAP. The Chief had one of his officers call the city public works department and get a couple big lights brought over. It was getting dark fast.

Once at Durango Police Headquarters, Jess and Buck were put in separate interview rooms. The officer escorting them asked if they needed anything and Buck asked for a bottle or can of Coke. Jess still had the water she was carrying when the whole incident started.

Detective Romero arrived at police headquarters on the heels of Christine Brewer, the District Attorney. She wanted to observe the interviews. Romero was extremely thorough. Even though Buck was very familiar with the Miranda Warning and understood his rights, Romero read him his rights and asked him if he wanted a lawyer. Buck declined and signed the letter waiving his right to counsel. Step by step Romero walked Buck through the events of the evening. Buck was impressed with Romero. He asked the right questions at the right time, he made copious notes on his note pad, even though the entire interview was being videotaped and he walked him through the events several times until he had a complete understanding of what happened.

Satisfied that he had everything he needed from Buck, Romero pushed back from the table stood up and turned for the door. He stopped turned and extended his hand toward Buck. Buck shook his hand. Romero said, "Buck, I'm glad it was them and not you." He opened the door and walked out. He followed the exact same procedure with Jess, including the handshake at the end.

By the time the interviews were over, the Chief, DA Brewer, Sheriff Sinclair and Detective Quinn were all standing outside the interview rooms. The Chief directed everyone into a small conference room and closed the door. He asked Romero to give them all a rundown of the interviews. Romero consulted his notes and then in clear strong voice explained that both interviews were consistent in their content, both agents had covered the events thoroughly and in his opinion, unless there was evidence to dispute the facts as he knew them, that he believed this was a good shooting.

Detective Quinn gave a recap of what had been discovered at the scene. Dani Walker, the Forensic Tech, had catalogued a total of fourteen rounds of various calibers. It was possible, he explained, that they might have missed something since the area was huge. Most of the bullets recovered had been found in vehicles in the parking lot. He also explained that he had gone over witness statements from those people they were able to interview and that their stories were consistent with the information just provided by Romero. He also concurred

that this was a good shooting. He then
mentioned that according to the
witnesses, Buck would probably be dead if
it wasn't for the fact that he kneeled at
the right time and that Jess was there.
Most of the rounds were directed at where
Buck was. Almost like the bad guys
hadn't even seen Jess.

He did make one note that got
everyone's attention. He said three of
the witnesses had asked him if they had
talked to the tall, blond guy. They all
felt that he had the best view from where
he was standing at the time. Quinn had
thus far been unable to locate a tall,
blond guy at the hotel.

The Chief then looked over at
Christine Brewer, the District Attorney,
and asked her for her opinion. She had
witnessed both interviews and was
satisfied that they had the full story.
She would recommend that no charges be
filed and the that the events of the
evening be classified a good shooting and
closed. Buck and Jess were to be
released.

Before they concluded, the Chief
told the group that he had been in
contact with the Sheriff in Teller County
and that the information Buck provided
about the case up there was accurate.
The Slattery brothers were the primary
suspects in the triple homicide. The
Teller County Sheriff had asked if it
would be OK if he sent two of his

detectives down to review the evidence
they had. The chief said he had allowed
that and that the detectives would arrive
sometime in the morning.

        His final comments were about the
preliminary findings of the Forensic
Pathologist. According to Dr. Kramer,
both men were hit multiple times.
Shooter A was hit in the lower torso and
in the neck, which would probably prove
to be the fatal wound, and shooter B was
hit three times in center mass. As a
side note, he had told the Chief to tell
both Buck and Jess that they had been
extremely accurate under the
circumstances and he was proud of them.
Smiles all around the table.

        "OK," said the Chief. "Let's get
Buck and Jess out of the interview rooms
and let's talk this through one time and
then get everyone out of here. It's
getting late and it's been a long night."

Chapter Thirty Seven

Buck and Jess joined the group. Handshakes and congratulations all around. Jess still looked a little shaken up and Buck tried valiantly to keep everyone from seeing his hands shake as he talked. Buck told them about walking towards the hotel entrance and seeing the tall, thin, blonde guy come out of the building and how something caused them each to stop and look at each other. Then Jess had called to him and as he turned towards her all hell broke loose. He asked if they had been able to interview the blonde and was told that no one could find him after the shooting.

Jess opened her laptop, pulled up the file she had sent him earlier and push the computer over towards Buck. "Is this the guy you saw?"

Buck, who hadn't had a chance to look at the file Jess had sent him, studied the picture. There were several pictures from his imprisonment in the military prison and it was in one those

pictures Buck spotted the special forces
tattoo. He was certain it was the same
guy. His mind flashed on the tattoo on
his right arm. The skull with the dagger
through it.

Buck looked up. "Ninety Eight
percent. I didn't realize it when I
first saw him, since it was just a
glance, but I remember seeing the tattoo
on his arm. I think that's what I first
focused on."

Terry Rubin, who had joined the
group a few minutes before asked. "Do
you think he set this up?"

Buck thought for a minute. "Don't
think so. He has never seen me, or Jess,
and I think it was just happenstance that
he was there at that time. I remember
thinking about how I was going to handle
the encounter when the shooters showed
up. It would have been obvious to him
that I was a cop. We were twenty feet
apart and my badge and gun were both
clipped to my belt."

The Sheriff looked around the
table. "Anything else before we head
out?"

Terry stood up. "I had a
conversation with the FBI computer guys.
We have a timeline now."

All eyes were on Terry as he
explained the conversations the computer
guys had picked up. He told them about
the conversation regarding slicing the

kid's throat and the little power play
that seemed to be going on. He talked
about the timeline being moved up to
Sunday morning.

Terry said, "I asked them to get
the transcripts to everyone and then I
headed home for a quick dinner. I knew
Buck had said he was going to dinner but
I wasn't sure where he was going so I
figured I'd give him time to eat. After
I finished dinner I was heading over to
his hotel to fill him in when the shots
fired call came over the radio."

Everyone kind of looked around the
table. Jess finally broke the silence.
"We don't have a lot of time to put this
together. We need to get moving."

The Sheriff looked at DA Brewer.
"Well, Chris, what do you think. We have
enough for a murder warrant at least?"

Brewer looked at Terry. "Get me
all the transcripts and the packet that
Jess sent Buck and send it to my office.
I will have my guys write up the warrant
and get it over to Judge Houseman. I
think we are on a good footing,
especially since there are other
outstanding warrants on this guy."

Jess spoke up. "I will call my
Director and see if we can get a search
warrant for the drugs. I think we have
enough to take it to a federal judge."

The Sheriff looked around. "OK
everyone. We got a lot to do. Buck,

Jess hang back a minute. OK? Everybody
else, let's get ready to put this to bed.
We will hook up in my office tonight at
seven and let's get all the SWAT team
leaders there as well. Thanks everyone.
Nice work tonight."

After everyone left the room, the
Sheriff and the Chief sat down and
pointed to the empty chairs. Buck and
Jess sat down. The Sheriff started the
conversation. "You guys were incredibly
lucky tonight. I am very glad you guys
weren't hurt. I stood at the scene where
Buck was kneeling and for the life of me
I can't figure out how you didn't get
hit. You've got one hell of a guardian
angel." She paused a beat.

"I just want to make sure you guys
are going to be OK. From the sound of
it, we are going to have a pretty big
operation going on and I need everyone in
top shape. If either of you feel you
might have trouble dealing with this it
is OK to step away now. I have already
spoken with both your directors and the
feeling all around is that you guys get
to make the call. I have a preacher and
a psychologist available at a moment's
call if you need to talk through this and
both the Chief and I are available for
you, too. So here it is. Are you good
to go?"

Buck looked at Jess and then back
to the Sheriff. "Good to go." He
responded.

The Sheriff looked at Jess. "Jess?"

Jess looked at Buck. "Good to go Ma'am."

The Sheriff looked at the Chief and then back to Jess and Buck. "OK then. You two get some sleep and let's meet up this afternoon."

She reached into her backpack and pulled out the two evidence bags containing Buck's and Jess's guns. She opened the bags and slid the guns and magazines back to their respective owners. Buck and Jess thanked the Sheriff and the Chief and headed for the door. A deputy was waiting to drive them back to their cars. He already had both their backpacks in the car since they had been dropped at the scene when all the shooting started. They drove back to the hotel in silence.

Chapter Thirty Eight

Blondy pulled his rental car into the truck yard, hit the bottom on the garage door opener for the smaller delivery door, drove up the ramp and pulled the car into the warehouse. He had been doing this every day since he arrived at the warehouse. He knew there were a lot of people looking for him and the less he was seen the better. The garage door rolled down and when it was closed he stepped out of the car.

Moustache headed over to him. "What the hell is going on out there? With all the sirens I thought for sure we were getting raided. I was getting ready to pull the plug and get the hell out of here!"

Blondy looked at him. "Damn, that was unreal! Felt like I was in a war zone again! Couple cops got into a shootout in the hotel parking lot. Damn bullets flying all over. I was like twenty feet away when the first shots rang out. Got my head down and headed for the car so I wouldn't get caught up in the lot when the cavalry arrived. God damn cops came from every direction. It was freakin nuts!" His whole body was shaking from the adrenalin rush.

Moustache looked at him with concern. "You think the cops were here for us or for the shooters?"

"Can't say for sure. I had this weird sensation, as the older cop was walking towards the hotel, that he actually stopped and looked straight at me, but then bullets started flying and I got the hell out of there."

"Anyone see you there?" Moustache asked. "They might be looking at you as a witness."

"Can't be sure. There were other people around. I am going to stay here until we head back to Mexico. Swing by my room when you go back to the hotel and grab my stuff."

Moustache filled him in on progress so far. They had filled the last half of the one trailer while he was gone and had just started on the last trailer. The last shipment of toys had also arrived and the kids were busy filling them up. He didn't see any problem making the deadline. He also let Blondy know that he had to up the amount of Oxy some of the kids were getting. They were running without sleep and some of them were starting to crash.

Blondy shook his head in agreement and headed for the office. He needed to sit down and get to his calm place. His body was still shaking. He closed the office door, sat in the chair, kicked back and stared at a spot on the ceiling. He focused every part of his being on that one spot. He had learned to do this from an old army Sergeant he had trained under during his first year with the Green Berets. At first, he thought it was bullshit, but after a while he found it got easier and easier to get to a calm place. That's what he was looking for now.

He thought about what Moustache had asked him. Was it possible the cops were aware of what was going on inside the ware house? He hadn't seen any signs that they were being watched, but he still had the twitch in his neck. The twitch was never wrong. The twitch had kept him alive in some of the most inhospitable places on earth and he always trusted the twitch. His mind started to focus in on the spot, his breathing became regular and he could feel his heartbeat returning to normal. But for some reason, he could not get the nagging feeling out of his head. They swept the warehouse three times a day with some of the most sophisticated anti-bugging software that was available. He never knew where Rojas got this stuff from but it was way high tech. So far, they had found no anomalies. Was it possible they missed something?

Then a weird thought crept into his psyche. Moustache was the one who ran the scans every day. Was it possible... No, he had to stop thinking like that. They had worked as a team a long time. But then again… Could he be working for someone else? Another cartel boss perhaps? Rojas had wiped out a lot of the other cartel bosses in his rise to the top, thanks to him and Moustache, but was it possible? Those guys had families and families sometimes have long memories. He decided that his thinking was wrong. He also decided to keep a closer eye on Moustache and the other guards, especially Rojas's nephew. Can't ever be too safe. The twitch hadn't gone away.

Chapter Thirty Nine

Buck and Jess thanked the deputy for the ride, grabbed their stuff and stepped out of the car into the early morning air. The air felt cool and Buck took a deep breath as the deputy drove off. He stood for a minute looking at the last of the stars as the dawn was starting to break. He looked at Jess.

"You OK?" He asked. "For real?"

Jess looked at him, tried to answer and wrapped her arms around him. Buck was surprised but he just let her hold him for a minute. He rested his hand on her back.

"It's OK." He said.

She let go of the bear hug, stepped back and looked at the ground. She wiped the tears from her eyes. "Look at me. What a mess." She said. "Big tough DEA agent and here I am crying like a little girl. What the hell is wrong with me?"

Buck just stood there for a minute. He wasn't quite sure what to say.

Finally, he said, "look Jess. None of us are perfect and we all deal with shit differently. I almost died tonight and if it wasn't for you, I probably would have. You saved my life and I am truly grateful."

He went on to tell her about the first bullet sailing just over his head when he knelt down. He hadn't mentioned how close it had come to anyone else. She looked at him and moved her hand up to her mouth. She hadn't realized how close it had come, either. Had he not dropped to his knees it would have hit him right in the chest and he wasn't wearing his body armor.

"What made you kneel?" she asked. "That was a strange reaction to the situation."

Bucked looked at her. "Not sure. I remember looking around for cover in that split second between seeing the guns and hearing the shot and I knew I needed to get small. If I had dove to the ground, I would not have been able to grab my gun and fire, so kneeling was the only option. I heard all those bullets flying by me and all I kept thinking about was that Lucy would kick my ass if I got myself killed."

His face almost lit up. He was never that spiritual, but there is no way he should have survived tonight. No way in hell. Yet here he was.

"Looks like Lucy and I did a good job keeping you alive." Jess replied.

There seemed to be an awkward moment coming so he pulled out his phone and pulled up his messages. He had eleven messages. Jess did the same and looked at the seven messages she had. Buck suggested they head inside and start returning messages and try to get some sleep. They agreed to meet at the Sheriff's office at one. Buck close his phone and nodded a silent thank you. Jess nodded back and they headed inside.

Chapter Forty

Buck opened the door to his room, stepped inside and locked the dead bolt. He walked over to the desk and set his gun and badge on the desk. The he sat on the edge of the bed and cried like a baby. He missed his wife so much and he would love to see her again, but getting killed today was not in his plans. Had Lucy reached out and helped him tonight? He had no idea, but every time he replayed the events of tonight in his head he got the same result.

The first bullet fired at him was definitely a kill shot. No doubt in his mind.   Had he not dropped to his knees, he would be lying on a slab. The first shot he fired just as his gun cleared the holster was way off the mark. A complete miss and the second two shots he fired, once he got both his hands on the gun and out in front of him, were off too. Or so he believed.   He could still see it as clear as while it was happening. He was tracking towards the shooter and pulled the trigger even though he was not lined

up. Pure muscle reaction. He was
certain the shots had missed, yet the
shooter went down. He ran it through his
mind several more times, each time more
and more certain he had not been on
target. He didn't know how to explain
it. Maybe Lucy was there tonight. He
did know one thing for certain. He owed
his life to Jess Gonzales.

Buck walked into the bathroom and
washed his face with cold water. He
dried off, pulled his phone out of his
pocket and sat down at the desk. His
first call was to his Director. Even
though the sun was barely up, he figured
his boss would be. He was right. The
Director answered right away.

"You OK?" he asked. No one says
hello anymore.

"Yes Sir." Buck replied. He went
on to tell him what happened, even though
he knew that the Director had already had
the same conversation with Sheriff
Sinclair. The Director listened
carefully, asked a couple questions and
then told Buck he was grateful that he
had survived. He then filled Buck in on
the interview with Claire Ringsby.

Claire Ringsby had been intercepted
just prior to boarding the flight to La
Guardia airport in New York. Tracy and
Doonen said she came along willingly.
Buck had worked with both Tracy and
Doonen on several occasions. Rachel
Tracy was a single mom with a ten-year-

old son. She worked mostly property
crimes, burglary and things like that.
Faith Doonen was a former basketball
player for the University of Colorado.
She was just short of six feet tall and
wore her hair short. Doonen typical
worked in cybercrimes.

        The Director continued. After the
initial shock of being pulled out of line
at the airport wore off, she opened right
up. Tracy and Doonen just had to sit
there and listen. According to her
statement, a couple weeks back a lawyer
from Denver, supposedly representing
potential trucking clients, walked into
the office and asked for one of the
owners. At the time Hector Vegas was the
only owner in the office and he met with
the lawyer. After the lawyer left the
office, Hector was very shaken up. She
didn't know what went on in the office
but later, when he told Dick Dillon about
the visit, Dick went nuts. She had never
seen them go at it like that as long as
she had worked there. Within a couple
days she was introduced to two guys, one
blonde, one Hispanic. They were
introduced as new partners. She was
afraid of them both. The warehouse was
walled off and she was no longer allowed
in the larger space. She seemed to have
no idea what was happening in the closed
off space. She just did her job and
hoped that neither one of the new
partners came into her office.

Two days ago, Dick took her aside, told her he had set up an offshore bank account for her and deposited fifty thousand dollars into it and he told her to finish up work that day and then disappear. She was afraid at this point, so she did what he said. Booked a flight out of town and headed to Denver. The impression Tracy and Doonen got was that Dick had not accepted the new arrangements and was planning to take his family and run. Hector, she told them, just looked nervous all the time. They said she seemed more concerned about her two bosses than herself. She also wondered if she would have to give the money back that Dick gave her.

"For the time being we have her stashed away in a hotel at the airport until we close this up. Bottom line, she doesn't seem to know much."

Buck responded. "Her statement lines up with what we have been speculating. The lawyer is a new angle. I have been wondering how they made contact. Can you get someone to check out the lawyer?"

"Already in the works. Denver Police are keeping an eye on Ringsby, I have the computer guys pulling everything they can find on the lawyer. Ringsby remembered his name and I have Tracy and Doonen sitting on his office."

"We probably don't have enough to get a warrant and we don't want to spook him or his bosses." Buck replied.

"Let's see what we can find out about him. The computer guys will pull his life apart and we will see what shakes out."

They talked for a few minutes about the raid for Sunday morning and the Director offered once again to send help. Buck told him he would let him know by the end of the day. They clicked off.

Buck looked at his messages and decided he needed to call his kids before returning any other calls. He dialed his daughter first. Cassandra was the middle child and she was every bit a middle child. In high school she played soccer, ran track and played volleyball. She lettered in all three sports. She was also the one who got in trouble for violating curfew, drinking, and whatever other mischief she could find to get into. Buck was surprised when she was accepted to the University of Arizona with a full scholarship for volleyball. He was even more surprised when she was accepted into law school. Cassie was never much for regimented education.

Two years ago, she suddenly dropped out of law school and her career path took a different track. She joined the Forest Service and was now working as a wildland firefighter with the Helena Hotshots. The Helena Hotshots were one of the elite firefighting teams based out of Helena, Montana. Buck was not surprised. He never saw her sitting behind a desk as a lawyer. She loved the outdoors and she was as tough as they come. Lucy wasn't pleased that she quit school without any discussion and she worried constantly whenever Cassie was called out on a fire, but she also knew her daughter and if this was where she was happy, then so was her mom.

Cassie's phone went straight to voice mail, so Buck figured she was probably on a fireline someplace. He left a message asking her to call him when she got the chance and to tell her that he loved her and missed her.

Next, he called David, his oldest son. David looked just like his dad at that age, he was slightly taller at six feet two and was a little heavier, but the resemblance was almost scary. David was a patrol officer with the Gunnison Police Department. He also played guitar in a local bluegrass/country band. David answered on the second ring. "Hey Dad, how are you?"

Buck spent a few minutes on pleasantries, how were the grandkids, how was the job going, the wife OK. Then he told him about the shootout. David had heard something on the news this morning as he was getting off shift but the reporter didn't have many details. He asked a few questions, was glad his Dad was OK and then they hung up, promising to get together soon.

Jason, his youngest son, answered the phone sounding like he was still half asleep. Jason was an architect and he lived in Boulder with his wife Kate and their three children. He listened in stunned silence as Buck told him about the shootout. Of all of Buck's kids, Jason was the one who had continued to follow Catholicism, just like his mom, and seemed to get more involved in his church after Lucy died. He told Buck that he believed that his mom had been there to watch over him. Buck asked him if he had heard from his sister. Since Jason and Cassie were closer in age, they had stayed the closest and typically spoke every week. He told Buck that the last he heard she was working on a fire in Northern California. They talked pleasantries for a few minutes then Buck signed off.

He felt a lot better after those calls. His family was important and they all stayed close. During the past year, since Lucy died, they had made an extra effort to include him in family things, and he was glad they had. It was the kids who kept him sane when in the beginning all he wanted to do was work and forget the pain of the loss. They were his rock.

Buck decided to wait on the other calls. He needed to put his head down on

the pillow and crash. For the first time
in his life he thought that maybe he was
too old for this kind of work. Even
though he had survived the encounter, he
was concerned that his reaction time was
off. His body began to shake and tears
formed in his eyes. He opened his wallet
took out the picture of Lucy and stared
at it for a few minutes. Before he put
it back into the sleeve in his wallet he
thanked her for looking out for him last
night. He laid back on the pillow and
went right to sleep.

       Down the hall, Jess got off the
phone with her Director. He, too, was
glad she had survived and based on the
information he had received, she had
handled herself in an extraordinary
manner and had done the DEA proud. He
was planning to put her in for a heroism
award. She told him that wasn't
necessary, but he insisted. They
discussed the planned raid and he offered
more assistance if needed, to which she
told him she would let him know if she
saw a need for more people. They also
discussed a few other operational things
that were in the works and he told her to
get some sleep and hung up.

       Jess stripped out of her clothes,
turned on the shower and stepped in. Out
of nowhere she was hit with a huge wave
of emotion and found herself sitting on
the floor of the shower with her arms
wrapped around her legs and the water
running down her head. She cried like

she hadn't ever cried before. By the
time she got out of the shower she was
emotionally drained and she was asleep as
soon as her head hit the pillow.

Chapter Forty One

Buck woke up with a start. He could hear something ringing in the distance, but he was unsure what it was. He looked around the room trying to focus on where he was. The phone continued to ring. Slowly his brain kicked into gear and he realized he was in his hotel room. He could also see sunshine coming through the gap in the curtains. He located the source of the ringing and picked up his phone. He recognized the number.

"Jimmy", He said. "What's up?"

"Jesus Buck. Are you alright? The Chief just stopped in for lunch and told me what happened."

Buck focused his clearing head. "Yeah, Jimmy. I'm Ok. It was a hell of a night. Thanks for asking."

"OK. Hearing your voice makes me feel better. So, you guys took out two bad guys in a shootout in a parking lot. Hell of a story to tell the grandkids. Someday."

"Yeah. Maybe not for a while though."

Jimmy laughed. "Listen Buck. The other reason I'm calling is that Dick Dillon is in here crying in his beer again. The Chief is keeping an eye on him until you can get here."

"OK. I will be there in fifteen. Don't let him leave."

"You got it." replied Jimmy.

Buck climbed out of the bed. Put on a clean pair of jeans and a clean t-shirt, clipped his badge and gun to his belt and grabbed his backpack. As he was walking through the front doors of the hotel he found himself slowing his pace and looking around the lot, carefully. Not seeing anything out of the ordinary, he headed for his car. As he neared his car, he called Terry Rubin.

"Hey Buck. Everything OK?" Terry asked.

"Yeah. You doing anything right now that can't wait?"

Terry replied. "Nothing that can't wait. What you got going on?"

"I am heading over to LaBon Café. Dick Dillon is there getting sauced. I want to take a run at him and see if we can confirm how many bad guys are on site and if Blondy is amongst them. You want in?"

Terry said, "hell yeah! I will meet you there, ten minutes."

Buck hung up and his phone rang. Number he didn't recognize.

"Buck Taylor."

"Agent Taylor. This is Detective Ronny Briscoe from Teller County."

"Hey Ronny. What's up?" said Buck.

"First off, the Sheriff said you had a shootout. Glad things turned out alright for you. Heard you put down our suspects. Thanks. I just wanted to let you know that we just got to the La Plata Sheriff's office and we are heading down to watch the autopsy on the Slattery Brothers. Wanted to thank you for closing this one up for us. Crime lab called this morning and they were able to pull a partial print off one of the bullets from Pop Grayson. It's a match for Mike Slattery. Case closed."

"That's great Ronny. Glad I could help."

"Listen Buck. Sheriff said to tell you that if you ever need anything, all you need to do is call. We owe you big. Thanks."

Buck thanked Ronny for the call and hung up. Another satisfied customer he thought to himself. He pulled out onto the highway and headed for the café.

Buck found a parking space a half block from the café, got out of his car and headed for the café. Terry Rubin and Durango Police Chief Chandler were standing outside the door to the café.

Chief Chandler said, "Hey Buck. You get any sleep? I spotted Dick Dillon when I stopped in for lunch. I knew you were thinking about talking to him, so I figured I would give you a call before he got too shitfaced."

Buck looked through the front door and saw Dick Dillon sitting at the end of the bar nursing a beer, a shot glass sat in front of him, half full of a slightly brown liquid. The bar was fairly crowded with lunch time patrons, but Buck didn't really want to wait. They were running out of time and Buck needed as much information as he could get.

Buck thanked the Chief, who said he would stand by at the front door, just in case Dick got belligerent. Terry and Buck walked into the bar and headed straight for Dick. Jimmy gave him a slight nod as he walked along the bar. If anything weird happened, he knew Jimmy would also have his back. Just as a precaution, he unsnapped the thumb break on his holster.

Terry grabbed the stool next to Dick and sat down. Buck stood next to Dick at the end of the bar. Jimmy looked at them both with droopy eyes.

"What the hell you guys looking at!" exclaimed Dick.

Buck started. "Hey Dick, my name is Buck and I work for the Colorado Bureau of Investigation and that's Terry, he works for the Sheriff. We'd like to talk to you for a minute about a couple things."

Dick sat up taller on his stool and with a couple slurred words said. "I don't have to talk to you, so get the hell out of my face." He started to get up from the stool, but Buck put his right hand on Dick's shoulder and gently, but firmly, held him in his place. Then Buck leaned his head down and whispered in Dick's ear.

"If you try to move again I am going to slam your face into the bar top. Then I am going to arrest you and let all these people sitting around us know that you and your partner allowed a Mexican drug cartel to get a foothold in their town."

Dick looked startled. Buck would swear that in that moment Dick went from falling down drunk to stone cold sober. Total waste of all the money he had spent to tie one on. Dick looked up at Buck.

"You can't do that?" He said rather meekly.

"Go ahead and try me." Said Buck in return.

Dick looked unsure of what to do next, so he leaned into the bar and took a sip of his beer. Buck wasn't sure if what happened next was just stupidity on Dick's part or if it was a smart move to protect himself and his family, but no matter what, Buck was ready. As Dick, holding the handle of his beer mug, started to swing the mug towards Bucks head, Buck reached out with his left hand and caught Dick's hand and the mug while at the same time, using his right hand, he drove Dick's face into the bar top. The crashing noise of Dick's face hitting the bar and the mug smashing into the floor made everyone in the bar jump. They all looked towards the end of the bar.

Several of the people sitting at the bar and the tables started to get up and head for the end of the bar. Jimmy smacked his sawed-off Louisville Slugger onto the bar top. Jimmy always kept the bat under the bar. Just in case. The crack it made when it hit the bar stopped everyone in their tracks. He just stared at everyone and slowly everyone sat back down in their seats.

Terry, who really hadn't expected the move, reached across Dick and held him down on the bar top. Jimmy started to move down the bar, but Buck held him off with a nod. By this time, Chief Chandler was at their side and had his handcuffs out. He reached past Terry, grabbed Dick's right arm, swung it behind him and put the cuff on his wrist. Buck slid the other arm around and the Chief did the same thing to that arm. Dick was bleeding all over the bar from what was probably a broken nose. Buck looked over at Jimmy and shrugged his shoulders. Jimmy just smiled and waved him off. Wasn't the first person who had ever face planted on Jimmy's bar and it wouldn't be the last.

Together Buck and Terry half carried and half dragged the semi-conscious Dick down the bar and headed for the door. The Chief had pulled out his radio and called for a patrol car for transport. Everyone in the bar watched silently. Once outside, Dick started to come to and started moaning about his nose. Jimmy had handed Buck a bar towel as they were getting ready to leave and he was holding the towel against Dick's nose. People on the street stopped and stared. It only took a minute for the patrol car to arrive and they loaded Dick in the back seat. Dick asked Terry to go with the police officer and to stop by the hospital on the way to the Sheriff's office and get Dick's nose taken care of. Buck would interview him later.

As the patrol car drove away the Chief looked at Buck. 'I gotta tell ya Buck. You sure have a way of keeping things interesting when you're in town."

Buck laughed. "Yeah and here I thought small town life was boring"

They both laughed. Buck told the
Chief he would let him know what Dick had
to say as soon as he could get him in the
interview room. He thanked the Chief for
his help, they shook hands and the Chief
headed back to his car. Buck stood there
for a minute. As he turned to walk back
to his car, his phone rang. Buck didn't
recognize the number, but he answered it
anyway.

Chapter Forty Two

"Buck Taylor."

"Hey Buck, It's Randall with the FBI. Wasn't sure when you were getting back here so I wanted to let you know the latest from the voice tap."

Buck got back to his car, opened the door and sat down on the seat. "Go ahead Randall."

"The guy with the southern accent got back to the warehouse just after your shootout in the parking lot. He told his friend all about it and told him that he was only a couple feet away when it all started. Since you saw him and can ID him and he saw the shootout and headed back to the warehouse, we can now definitively place him in the warehouse. He said he was going to stay in the warehouse until they head back to Mexico and he asked the other guy to get his stuff from the hotel."

"That's great Randall. I am heading to the Sheriff's office now."

"Oh, one more thing. The other guy mentioned that he had to up the dose on the kids since they hadn't had any sleep and some of them were crashing. If that is true, then we can confirm that those kids are being drugged to keep them there. I gave this to the Sheriff and the DA and they are going to add kidnapping and illegal imprisonment to the charges on the warrant."

Buck thanked Randall, hung up and sat back in his seat. This confirmed what he already believed. Those kids had been tortured and drugged, probably with Oxy, and in all likelihood, have no idea where they even are. They are like zombies. The more he thought about it the more pissed he got. Then a new thought creeped into his head. Once ICE took those kids into their possession they would most likely be transported to a holding facility in Alamosa and then transported to either Tucson or Houston where they would await deportation. They would be prisoners again, this time courtesy of Uncle Sam. He was having a real problem with that. These kids had been through enough.

Buck pulled up a number on his phone and then stared at it for a couple minutes. Buck was definitely a law and order person and he was not a fan of illegal immigration, but this was something else. These kids never asked to come here and the idea of keeping them as prisoners until they were deported back to almost certain death was more than he could fathom. Once Rojas found out that his distribution dreams had been dismantled, he would have his revenge on everyone he could get to, and that would probably include these kids. Their lives were in serious danger if they were sent back to Mexico.

Buck dialed the number. If word of what he was about to do got out, his credibility with the Feds would go right out the window. It was a risk he was willing to take. His thought, just before the Director answered his phone, was that Lucy would approve. He was doing the right thing.

"Hey Buck", the Director answered. "What's up?" Someone finally said hello.

Buck gave the Director an update on what they had gotten off the voice tap and about the incident with Dick Dillon, then he got to the real reason for the call.

"Sir, do you have a phone number for that human rights lawyer, the one who gave the talk on human trafficking at the police conference a few months back?"

"Are you talking about Sandi Calhoun?" asked the Director.

"Yes sir, I think that was her name."

"What's going on Buck?"

Buck explained about the kids being drugged and held prisoner and that he was concerned that unless someone stepped in that they were just going it be imprisoned someplace else.

When he finished, the Director was silent. Finally saying, "Buck. What are you planning on doing if I get you her phone number?"

"Well Sir. I'd rather not say. I don't want to get you involved and the less you know the better. If the shit hits the fan with the Feds, I will take the heat. This is my move."

Silence. Anyone who knew Buck would know that he would not knowingly circumvent the law and the Director, more than anyone else, knew that Buck did not take things like this lightly.

"I'll tell you what I am going to do. The Governor knows her quite well. They worked on several anti-trafficking bills when he was in the legislature. I am going to call him and see if he will call her and ask her to call you. If the shit hits the fan, he can cover for both of us. He never passes up an opportunity to thumb his nose at the federal government and this could be a huge humanitarian feather in his cap come the next election."

"Do you think he will do it?" Buck asked.

"Are you kidding? He is still pissed about the whole sanctuary city thing the feds tried to pull on Denver. He would do this in a heartbeat. Answer your phone when it rings." The Director hung up.

Buck headed back to the Sheriff's office.

Chapter Forty Three

The Sheriff's office was buzzing with activity. In the conference room the three SWAT Commanders, La Plata County, DEA and FBI, had one of the construction plans for the warehouse and the site pulled up on the big screen at the front of the room. Sitting around the room were twenty-five SWAT team members. The FBI SWAT Commander was walking the teams through various breaching strategies. He was pointing out the possible breach points into the building. Buck stepped into the room and stood in the back so as not to get in the way.

There were three breach points circled in red on the screen; the front door to the office, the smaller roll-up delivery door at the front of the building and the rear door, which would hopefully give the teams access to the cage area. The commander was pointing out that all the doors opened out or in the case of the delivery door rolled up. The office door was ninety percent glass

so that one would be easy to shatter. At
six AM in the morning they were not
expecting anyone to be in the office.

     It was decided after a lengthy
discussion that part of the FBI team
would breach the office. At the same
time the La Plata team, with the help of
the additional FBI SWAT guys, would use
one of the heavy personnel carriers to
smash through the delivery door. They
knew from surveillance that the roll-up
door was electric and that they would be
unlikely to raise it from outside.
Immediately upon crashing thru the door,
the breach team would lob in a couple
flash bang grenades to cause a
distraction and hopefully disable the
guards.

     One of the big concerns with using
the flash bangs was the presence of the
kids. They would be unprotected and
would probably feel the full effects. No
one was happy about that but there was no
other way to breach and disable the
guards safely and they didn't want the
guards shooting the kids. Unfortunately,
it was an acceptable risk.

     At the same time as the two front
of the building breaches were taking
place, the DEA would use an explosive
charge and blow the rear door. Part of
the DEA team would also remain outside
the facility after the breach to pick up
any runners.

The FBI Commander reminded everyone that the first priority was to protect the kids inside. The rules of engagement were simple. Take whatever steps were needed to protect the kids and the SWAT teams from being harmed by the guards. This was going to be a tall order.

After a little more discussion everyone agreed with the plan and the Sheriff got up from her seat and stood behind the podium.

"First, I want to thank you all for your help with this. We have never been involved in anything of this magnitude and we appreciate all the work you have done and will do to make this raid a success. I want to go over a few more operational details so we are all on the same page. Even though this is a joint operation involving multiple agencies, it was decided after discussion with all those agencies that the Sheriff's Office will be in operational control. Terry Rubin, my narcotics investigator and the guy who got this all rolling, will be in tactical command. I will be right there with him at the command center. So you are all aware, the command center will be established in the auto body shop across the street from the warehouse. We have been using this for our surveillance and it will give us good visibility. The other person in the command center will be Buck Taylor. Buck is standing in the back corner and he is with the Colorado Bureau of Investigation. Buck is pretty

much the reason you are all here
tonight."

Everyone turned and looked at Buck,
who gave a slight nod of his head.

The Sheriff continued. "At five AM
we will leave this office and stage in
our respective areas. Access to the
warehouse property will be through the
back corner of the fence. The FBI sneak
and peek team used that access for their
entry into the complex. Once inside,
teams will take up positions at their
assigned entry points. The FBI team will
be responsible to disengage the
electronic lock on the front gate and
clear the way for the breaching vehicle.
The breaching vehicle will stage at the
end of the street out of sight of the
warehouse. There will be two FBI snipers
on the roof of the body shop and two more
on the roof of the building behind the
warehouse. They will be designated
overwatch one and two respectively." The
Sheriff used a laser pointer to point to
both locations on the big screen, as well
as, the back entry point.

"The La Plata SWAT team is
designated Team Able, FBI SWAT is Team
Baker and DEA SWAT is Team Charlie. My
Patrol division will block off all the
streets surrounding the warehouse at
fifteen minutes before the raid. Durango
Police will set up a roadblock at the
same time on US 550 south and north of
the warehouse. There will be Colorado

State Troopers stationed south and north of the city on 550 and west and east of the city on 160. They will be there to stop any of the trucks that might leave the yard before we are ready. The FBI computer team has all the trailers GPS tagged and will keep us apprised of any early movement. The Southern Ute Tribal Police will cover 550 south of the city if any of the trucks should make it onto reservation territory. They will be backed up by the New Mexico State Police. Any questions so far?"

The Sheriff looked around the room. No questions from the teams.

She continued. "Once we have breached the warehouse all focus must be on the safety of the kids. The guards are to be disabled in any way that makes sense and does not put any of you folks in harm's way. We know there are at least six armed individuals on site. It is possible there are others we are not aware of, but we have tried to identify them all. While all of this is happening on site, the Durango Police along with several members of the FBI will be executing a "No Knock" warrant on one Hector Vegas. He is one of the owners of the trucking company. The other owner, thanks to Buck Taylor, is already in our custody and as soon as he is finished up at the hospital he will be put in a cell." Everyone again looked at Buck and many of those in the room smiled and nodded their approval.

"One other item, just so you all have the full picture. CBI will also be executing a "No Knock" warrant this morning on a cartel lawyer in Denver. As you can see this is a wide-ranging operation. If we can successfully shut this down, we will put a huge kink in the distribution network of the cartels. Please be careful. The people on site at the warehouse are incredibly dangerous. Jessica Gonzales the DEA Agent in Charge of the Grand Junction office would like a minute."

Terry Rubin entered the room, stood next to Buck and softly said. "Dick is in the interview room as soon as you are ready. He has a broken nose and slight concussion, but the emergency room doctor said he should be fine." Buck nodded. Jess Gonzales walked up to the podium.

"Good evening. This operation is huge. If this distribution network is as big as we assume, it will be months before we know the impact we will make after the raid. We will document every move we make. Make sure your body cameras are fully operational. We don't want some lawyer screwing up our good work. Once the space is secure, my team will immediately start documenting the evidence with the help of the FBI Forensic team. Evidence gathering is important, but the safety of the kids and our teams is priority one. Be safe and be careful." Jess sat back down in her chair.

Terry Rubin walked to the front of the room and stood behind the podium. "For those of you I haven't met, I am Terry Rubin with the La Plata County Sheriff's Department. I have been asked to be in tactical command of this operation. I don't want to go back over everything we have covered so far. Check your gear and communications equipment. We will reassemble back here at four AM to go over any final details. We want everyone to go home tomorrow after we are finished. So be safe."

"One more thing. SWAT will take control of all the kids until ICE can get onsite.   We have ICE staging just outside of town, so they wouldn't be in the way during the raid. We will have medical help and several ambulances available since some of these kids might be starting to go through withdrawal. As soon as we can clear everyone at the scene, we will transport the kids by bus to here, where we will begin interviews. At this point we still don't know who is who inside the warehouse so until we clear each person, everyone is a suspect."

The meeting broke up and the SWAT Commanders separated into teams to discuss the actual onsite procedures in more detail. Several of the SWAT members from the various units had worked with Buck in the past and they stopped at the back of the room to congratulate him on the shootout and to talk about how he managed to survive. Buck recounted the events and many of the team members just scratched their heads as they listened. Jess Gonzales joined the group and corroborated Buck's telling of the events.

As the group broke up, Jess took Buck aside. "Did you get any sleep?" she asked.

Buck replied. "A little. You?"

"I didn't sleep much, but I think I am doing OK."

Buck looked at her. "Why don't you stay with us in the command center until the raid is over? Let your SWAT guys handle it."

"I may take you up on that offer. Hey, I heard you had a little more excitement this afternoon at some bar. Broke a guy's nose. You are one bad ass, Buck Taylor."

Buck smiled. "Yeah, takes a real bad ass to take down a drunk." He laughed, as did Jess.

Just then Terry Rubin came through the door. "I've got Dick in interview one."

"Excellent. Let's go see if he wants to cooperate. Can you find the DA and have her meet us there? I'd like her to observe." Terry headed to find the DA, just as Buck's phone rang.

Chapter Forty Four

Buck pulled out his phone. Unknown number. Buck answer the call.

"Buck Taylor."

"Agent Taylor, this is Sandi Calhoun. Are you able to talk?"

Buck asked her to hold on for a second and he headed out the side door and into the parking lot. Once clear of the building he reestablished the call.

"Yes, Ma'am and thanks for calling me back."

"I must say Agent Taylor that this seems quite unusual. I don't often get a call from the Governor asking me to call a police officer and to keep the conversation totally off the record. I will also say that the Governor told me that you are highly respected and that whatever you tell me, I can count on. Now would you mind telling me what this is all about."

"Yes Ma'am. I have a problem that I think might be right up your alley."

Buck proceeded to tell her as much about the raid as he felt comfortable talking about with a civilian. He then got to the heart of the conversation.

"These kids have been drugged and tortured for God knows how long. I am worried that once ICE takes control of them they are going to end up in a detention facility with minimal medical help. I am hoping you might be able to work something out to get them the help they need in someplace other than a prison. These kids, as far as we know, haven't done anything wrong and they probably have no idea that they are someplace other than Mexico. They will be scared, most likely traumatized after the raid and many will be starting withdrawal."

There was silence on the other end of the phone as Sandi Calhoun tried to wrap her head around what Buck had just told her. She finally replied.

"Agent Taylor, how many young men and women are we talking about?"

"We do not know for sure, but we think it could be as many as thirty or thirty-five. We also have no idea of their ages. One other thing you should know. Some of the girls have been sexually assaulted while in captivity."

"Oh my God." Sandi replied. "Agent Taylor, the Governor said that it is totally out of character for you to do this and he will take full responsibility for the information getting to me. But I would like to know for my own peace of mind, why are you doing this?"

Buck thought for a minute. "Well Ma'am, I'm not quite sure. I have a real problem with kids being abused, no matter where they are from, and these kids have been through hell. I guess I just don't want them to be hurt anymore. To be totally honest with you, if these kids get sent back to Mexico their chances of survival are pretty much non-existent. This is one of the worst cartels we have ever seen."

"Good answer, Agent Taylor. I am going to hang up and make believe this call never happened. I will do everything I can to see that these kids are treated fairly and given the chance for asylum, if that is what they want. I will not contact you directly unless it is something important, but know that this has my full attention. Thank you, Agent Taylor." Sandi Calhoun hung up.

Buck was a little conflicted. He did what he believed was the right thing to do but he also did something that as a cop he shouldn't have done and that was get a lawyer involved. He put away his phone and just stood there for a moment all alone in the parking lot.

He dialed the Director, who answered on the second ring. "Hello Buck. What's going on?" He said Hello.

Buck filled him on the raid details and then said, "I just spoke to the lawyer. She sounds like she is onboard."

The Director replied. "That's great news. The Governor will be pleased and from this moment on, I have no idea what you are talking about."

Buck asked. "Are you ready to go after the cartel lawyer?"

The Director replied. "Warrants are in place. I have a team on his residence and a team on his office. We've been sitting on both locations but so far, we haven't seen him at either location. We are hoping he hasn't rabbited. We issued an All-Points Bulletin on him and his car and we alerted Homeland and TSA in case he heads for the airport. They have flagged his license and passport."

"Thanks Sir. I need to get back inside to interview one of the owners of the trucking company."

"Hey Buck? Be careful tomorrow. I don't want to lose you."

Buck hung up and was just about to enter the building when his phone rang again. This time it was Hank Clancy, FBI.

"Hey Hank. What's up?"

"Great news Buck. First, we have all the warrants in place. Copies are being sent electronically to the Sheriff as we speak. Second, we were finally able to ping the encrypted sat phone at the other end of the call. We have a location on Carlos Rojas."

"That's great news Hank. Any chance we can get to him?"

"Not likely," replied Hank. "He is living in a huge hacienda about forty miles south of the border, south of New Mexico. The hacienda used to belong to that Mexican American movie producer, Simon Rivera and is in the middle of nowhere."

Buck thought for a minute. "Isn't that the guy who disappeared a couple years back with his entire family?"

"One in the same, Buck. Everyone always assumed he bolted to avoid a huge tax bill the IRS was planning to drop on him. Maybe we were wrong and him and his family are buried somewhere out in the desert."

"Jesus, that takes balls, to kill someone and then move into their house."

"You are right, Buck. Who knows what goes on in this guy Rojas's head. Hopefully, we will cripple his operation enough that the other cartels, what's left of them, will figure out a way to retaliate against him. Would be good for us."

"You got that right", replied Buck.

"Alright, I need to run so I can meet with the forensics team. We will arrive by military transport right at dawn and will stage at the airport until we get the all clear from you to come in. Good luck tomorrow and keep your head down."

Hank hung up. Buck headed upstairs to interview one.

Chapter Forty Five

Dick Dillon was sitting handcuffed to the table in interview room one when Buck opened the door. He had a bandage covering his broken nose and the start of what were going to be two amazing black eyes. He was holding his head, either from the pain of the slight concussion or the pain of the hangover he was most likely starting to experience. He looked up as Buck entered the room.

"Hey. I ain't talkin to you. You broke my damn nose." His words were muffled by the bandage and the cotton that had been stuffed up his nostrils to stop the bleeding. Buck just smiled and sat down opposite Dick. Opening a manila folder, Buck took out his Miranda card and read Dick his Miranda warning. When he was finished reading the warning he asked Dick if he understood his rights. After several attempts, Dick finally acknowledged he understood his rights.

"You have no one to blame but yourself. I told you what was going to happen if you got smart with me, so you had to test it." Buck hesitated for effect. "Or was that your plan from the minute I walked up to you. Get yourself locked up so we could protect you."

A muffled voice. "I don't know what you're talkin about. Why don't you go bother someone else and leave me alone? I'm gonna sue you guys for breakin my nose."

"No problem, Dick." Buck said. "We will let you go as soon as you tell us about the cartel taking over your business and setting up a drug distribution network in your hometown. Your neighbors are going to love hearing about that."

Dick looked angry. "You don't know anything, so why don't you get out of my face and get me a lawyer."

"Good idea, Dick. Maybe we can call that cartel lawyer that you and Hector went into business with. I'll bet his boss will be really happy when he tells him you have been arrested and are cooperating with us."

Dick suddenly went ashen. "You can't do that. I haven't told you anything."

"That's true Dick, you haven't told us anything. But we have been tapping your phones and computers for a couple days now and once we let that information slip to your attorney, the big cartel boss is going to think it came from you."

Buck pushed his chair back and stood up to leave. "I'm going to call your attorney. I hope you have a way to protect your family. Cartel guys don't mess around."

Dick suddenly lost all his fight. "Wait. I don't want my family hurt. On second thought, I don't want a lawyer. Ask me what you want."

"OK Dick. Why don't you start from the top and I will fill in the blanks as we go?"

Dick started from the beginning when he first heard about the cartel lawyer. He told Buck how he lost his temper with Hector and how they almost got into a fist fight that afternoon in the office. He told him how he hated the idea, how he hated the money and how he gave part of the money away to Claire Ringsby, his office manager, so she could get out of town. He told Buck he was working on a plan to get him and his family out of town as well. He also told Buck, reluctantly, of being knocked down by Blondy when he asked what they were doing in the sealed off portion of the warehouse. He figured it had to be drugs, but he never got to see inside the space.

He wanted Buck to believe that he wanted no part of what was going on, but that Hector seemed to be starting to come around to working with the cartel guys. He told Buck he was afraid for his family's safety and the only reason he tried to hit Buck in the bar was because he had too much to drink and his inebriated mind thought if he got himself arrested he might be able to protect his family. After about forty minutes, he stopped talking and answering questions, put his head in his hands and cried.

Buck sat back in his chair. During the conversation, Buck had shown Dick the picture of Harry Crank and Dick identified him as the blond guy in the warehouse. He looked almost petrified when he saw the picture.

"Alright Dick. You did really good. In a few minutes a Deputy is going to bring in a copy of everything we just talked about. I need you to sign the statement after you read it and make sure it is what you told me."

Dick looked up and tried to wipe the tears from his eyes with his hands still in handcuffs. "What's going to happen to my family? Can you protect them?"

"For right now, we are going to put you back in a cell. You are being held for assaulting a police officer. Tomorrow morning, the FBI will execute a search warrant on your house. At that point, it will be up to the feds how they are going to deal with you and your family. If what you have told me is true, it might be possible for your lawyer to get you into witness protection. That's not my call. Continue to cooperate and we will see what happens. I am going to have the DA get you a public defender for now. Just sit tight."

Buck got up from the chair and when the door buzzed he opened it and stepped out. The Sheriff and DA were waiting.

Buck looked at the DA. "Do we have what we need to execute the warrants?"

DA Brewer responded. "I think we are golden. I will call the Public Defender as soon as I leave here and explain the situation. We will make sure they keep this under wraps until after the raid."

The Sheriff looked at Buck. "You think we can get the FBI to recommend witness protection?"

"I will talk to Hank Clancy in the morning and get his take. In the meantime, can you call Durango PD and have them put someone on Dick's house until this is all over? Let's try to keep his family safe."

"You got it Buck. Why don't you go get some dinner and we will see you back here in a couple hours?"

The Sheriff and DA Brewer walked out together, and Buck headed for the

back door. He needed some air and a good
meal. One of Jimmy Palumbo's burgers
would probably fit the bill.

Chapter Forty Six

It was high summer tourist season in Durango and the sidewalks, shops and restaurants were packed with people. Buck had to go over three blocks before he could find a parking space. He pulled in and sat for a minute and just watched all the people. Buck was a student of human nature and he thought back on the days when the family would take driving vacations and in small towns all over the west, just like this one, Buck would watch the people on the streets and make up stories about them for the kids. He could keep the kids entertained for hours and even weeks later, long after the vacation was over, the kids would still make mention of the characters Buck had described. He found himself in a melancholy moment as he thought about his life with Lucy. His eyes got moist and he wiped them with the back of his hand.

Buck took out his phone and dialed his daughter Cassie. He expected to get her voice mail and was ready to leave a message when she answered the phone.

"Dad are you alright? I just came in out of the field and got Jason's voicemail and was just getting ready to dial your number. A shootout, Oh my God."

"I'm OK Cass", Buck replied. "It could have been worse."

"Dad, Jason said all the shots were directed at you and that mom protected you. Is he joking?"

"Well, some of that is true. Most of the shots did come my way and I am alive and unscathed. I don't know if your mom was looking out for me or what. Must have just been my lucky day."

"What happened to the guy who was shooting at you? Did you arrest him?"

"Well, not quite. There were actually two shooters." Buck paused a minute.

"Dad, what happened to the shooters?"

"Both shooters are dead. I got one and Jess Gonzales, you remember Jess, she works for the DEA, she took out the other one."

Cassie was silent for a second. "I'm so sorry Dad. It must have been horrible. I'm glad Jess had your back."

"Yeah, me too. Listen kiddo, I need to go. I have to work tonight and need to get some food. You stay safe OK and we can talk in a couple days if you have some time."

"OK Dad. Try to stay out of harm's way, OK. Love you, Dad."

"Love you too Kiddo."

Buck hung up and just sat for a minute. The he shut of the car, climbed out and headed for the La Bon Café.

The café was packed to the doors, but as soon as Jimmy saw Buck he pulled his stool from behind the bar and set Buck up on the end of the bar. Once again, he didn't ask what Buck wanted. He dropped a huge slab of meat on the grill and brought over a bottle of Coke.

"Hey, man. How's Dick Dillon? Man did you slam him."

Buck smiled. "Broken nose and a mild concussion. Hey, sorry about the mess on the bar."

"No worries, man. Not the first time somebody bled on the bar. Won't be the last." Jimmy laughed a hearty laugh. He walked off, flipped Buck's burger, dropped a handful of fries into the hot oil and headed to the end of the bar to refill some glasses. He walked back to the grill, put a big chunk of cheddar cheese on the burger, delivered another burger to someone half way down the bar and then put the burger on the bun, piled on the fries and delivered the plate to Buck.

"Enjoy, man." Then Jimmy headed off to take care of the rest of his customers.

Buck dug in like he hadn't eaten in days. The noise level in the narrow space was intense but Buck loved the environment and Jimmy looked like he was truly in his element. Jimmy worked the room like a politician, shaking hands with newcomers, filling glasses, flipping burgers. It was a sight to see. It was also the first time Buck had seen Jimmy handle the bar on a busy night without Loraine. He would have to tell her what a great job Jimmy did while she was gone.

Buck finished his burger and fries, put the cap on the bottle of coke and dropped a twenty dollar bill on the bar. Jimmy was having a spirited conversation with another biker down the bar, so he just waved to Jimmy as he left. He walked out into the night and headed for the car.

This was the time of night when Buck missed Lucy the most. Whenever he was on an assignment out of town, he would always call her at nine o'clock. They would talk about how her day went and he would always assure her that he would be OK, even though there was never a guarantee. As her disease progressed he always tried to minimize the worry for her and tried to keep the conversation

light. He missed wishing her a good
night. As he slipped into the car, his
focus switched over. He let the
melancholy go and put his head in what he
liked to call mission mode. He focused
all his attention on what was coming up
in the next couple hours. He pulled out
of the parking space and headed for the
Sheriff's office.

Chapter Forty Seven

Buck pulled into the parking space right opposite the side door of the Sheriff's office, grabbed his backpack and headed inside to the conference room. His first stop was to talk to Randall from the FBI sneak and peek team. Randall was busy listening to his headphones and typing furiously on his computer. Buck tapped him on his shoulder. Randall held up one finger to indicate he needed a second. He finished typing and pulled off his headphones.

"Sorry Buck. Wanted to make sure I got that final conversation transcribed for Agent Clancy. What's up?"

"Anything new on the taps?"

Randall slid his computer over so Buck could get a better look at the screen and scrolled back up to the top of the most recent page. Buck read what Randall had transcribed. There were no new earth shattering revelations. What he read sounded like a group of people trying to wrap up a project. Lots of activity, very little conversation. Buck finished reading.

Randall spoke first. "We checked texts earlier and all the drivers responded back that they would be onsite by four AM."

Buck responded. "Awesome. This thing is coming to an end. Any word from the NSA on the encrypted laptop?"

"No, sir. Agent Clancy has given our SWAT guys orders to grab all the computer equipment they can find. He wants it shipped immediately after the raid to the NSA at Fort Meade. They are thinking they might have better luck breaking the encryption if they have the machines on site."

"Has Terry Rubin asked you if you are able to block all the bad guys communications during the raid? Is that possible from here?"

"No Sir." He hasn't discussed it with me. He might have spoken with Josh or Toby. The answer to your question is, yes. We can shut down their entire network from right here."

"Good." Replied Buck. "Let's kill everything as soon as the word is given to breach the warehouse. Also, have the Colorado and New Mexico State Troopers and the Southern Ute Tribal Police been given access to the GPS tags on the trailers so they can track them if they leave before we hit the warehouse?"

"Yeah. The Sheriff and Terry had a
conference call with all three agencies a
little bit ago. We gave them each access
to a secure cell phone app that they can
use to track the trailers."

Buck thanked Randall and headed off
to find the Sheriff and Terry Rubin.
They were both sitting comfortably in the
Sheriff's office. The Sheriff waved Buck
in.

Buck said. "I just spoke with
Randall and asked him to shutdown all
communication from inside the warehouse
as soon as we are ready to breach. He
said you guys have already spoken to
Colorado, New Mexico and the Tribal
Police and they have access to the GPS
tags on the trailers."

Terry replied. "Great idea on the
communications. It never crossed my
mind. Yes. Everyone has the tags and
access to a cell phone app Randall had.
They are all ready and will have their
units stationed per our discussion by
five AM. They will not move to intercept
any of the trucks until you give the
word."

"Excellent. I'm going to check in
with SWAT. Oh, remember, you are in
tactical command of this operation, so
you will be the one to let our partners
on the road know when they can move on
the trucks. Are you up for all this?"

Terry smiled. "Yes sir. You can count on me."

The Sheriff smiled and nodded her head in agreement. Buck looked at Terry.

"I have no doubt you are ready. The Sheriff and I will be right there with you, but you know what needs to happen and I am confident you can do this."

"Thanks Buck. I really appreciate that. Means a lot coming from you."

Buck nodded and headed out the door. He found the three SWAT Commanders in his temporary office leaning over the desk, studying the blueprints they had gotten from the building department.

"You guys ready?" Buck asked.

The FBI Commander looked up from the blueprints. "Ready as we can be. We were just going over this again. Sure wish we had an easier way to breach the space. We are worried about the time between blowing the rear door, crashing into the cargo door and setting off the flash bangs. The bad guys may have enough time to start spraying those kids."

Buck looked at the blue print. "Are you planning to kill the power to the space just before we hit it?"

The Sheriff's SWAT Commander responded. "We talked about it, but then we are going in blind with possibly forty

people running around in a panic. We
could miss one of the bad guys and end up
getting someone killed"

     The DEA SWAT Commander spoke up.
"The other concern is that the roll-up
door could crash down on the assault
vehicle and block our access into the
warehouse. That would put all the burden
of the breach on my guys coming in the
back door. Not great."

     Buck pointed to the door that had
been drawn between the office and the
warehouse space. "We don't know exactly
where this door is, but what would happen
if we made a stealth entry into the
office and breached through this door?
Can you do that?"

     They all looked at Buck. "Great
minds." Said the FBI Commander. "That's
what we were just talking about as you
walked in. We can pick the lock on the
office door instead of breaking it. The
office should be empty. We can clear it
quickly and then set up on the inner
door. If it opens into the space, we are
golden. If it opens into the office, we
still have a timing issue, but not as
bad."

     Buck stood up. "Let me find out."
And he walked out the door and headed
down the hall to the holding cells.

     Dick Dillon was not happy to see
Buck walking towards his cell. His head

and nose still hurt like hell. Buck stopped at the cell door.

"The door the cartel guys installed in the wall they built between the office and the warehouse. Which way does it open? Into the warehouse or into the office?"

Dick scratched his head and thought real hard. "It opens into the warehouse."

"Are you absolutely sure?" Buck asked.

"Yeah. No doubt."

"Thanks." Buck headed back down the hall leaving Dick to wonder what that was all about. The SWAT Commanders were still where he left them.

"According to the owner we have in custody, the door opens into the warehouse."

"That will work", said the FBI Commander. "Now all we have to do is get into the office without them hearing us. This just improved our chances of keeping those kids alive. Nice work Buck. Thanks."

Buck nodded. "Always happy to help." He walked out of the office to find another bottle of Coke. It was gonna be a long night, so he decided to find a quiet corner in the conference room and take a nap.

Chapter Forty Eight

Buck's internal alarm clock went off at three forty-five AM and he sat up and tried to stretch the kinks out of his back and shoulders. Sleeping in chairs was for younger folks. He thought to himself. "I'm getting too old for this crap." He took a long gulp out of what was left of his bottle of Coke, tossed the empty into the recycle bin in the corner and stood up. Both knees creaked like they really objected to waking up from sleeping in a chair.

Josh was now working at the listening station and transcribing his notes as he listened to the taps. He looked up as Buck approached gave him a thumbs up signal and went back to typing. Buck headed for the ground floor.

The SWAT guys had started to arrive and were busy checking their gear. Everyone was dressed in black from head to toe. Ballistic vests were being put on and communications gear was being checked and rechecked. Each SWAT member

had a balaclava wrapped around his neck
for easy access to conceal their faces
during the raid. Helmets were put on and
then weapons were checked. Pistols were
holstered, and assault rifles were
connected to a lanyard hanging around
each person's neck.

Outside in the parking lot, the
breachers were checking their fuses and
setting up the quantities of Semtex they
believed they would need. Buck was
surprised at the lack of noise. Each
team member knew his or her job as well
as the jobs of the rest of the team. If
one person was to fall, everyone on the
team knew how to pick up the slack.

Each team member also checked their
medical pouch. They all carried a modest
supply of first aid supplies. In
situations like they were about to enter,
if someone was hurt, seconds counted.
They all understood the risks and they
were all well prepared for what lay
ahead.

Buck walked over to his Jeep and
opened the rear hatch. First, he
unlocked the secure lockbox that was
welded to the rear floor. He removed a
tactical thigh holster, removed the semi-
automatic pistol, dropped the magazine
and check the bullets. He replaced the
magazine and racked the slide. He then
flicked the safety on and holstered the
weapon. He then checked the three other
spare magazines and replaced each one

back in its assigned slot. He grabbed his ballistic vest and slipped it over his shoulders, slid the zipper up and checked to make sure he had his extra handcuffs and a supply of flex cuffs, his flashlight and a couple additional magazines all loaded with forty-five caliber shells. He placed his expandable baton in the holder at the side of the vest. Checking to make sure he had everything he needed, he slipped on his thin black nylon jacket, emblazoned with CBI in large letters on both the back and the left side front. He covered his head with a CBI ball cap and shut the rear hatch.

As he headed back to the building he ran into Jess Gonzales. From their clothes and equipment, they could have been twins, except Jess's vest was emblazoned with DEA. She also carried a Taser attached to the left side of her belt. She would normally wear the Taser on her right hip, so it was instinctively the first weapon she would grab. Tonight, was different. Tonight, the rules of engagement were different and the situation more dangerous.

"Hey Jess. You ready?"

"You bet Buck. The teams are loading up and we are ready to roll out. Hey listen, things are going to get a little crazy later and if I don't have a chance to say it, thanks for calling me in on this one."

"No worries, Jess. Wouldn't want anyone else at my side."

Jess nodded and headed for the SUV that her SWAT team was climbing into.

Terry and Sheriff Sinclair walked up to Buck. Everyone was in plain clothes and everyone was weaponed up.

"Buck", Terry spoke. "You ready to head over to the command center?"

Buck nodded and they all headed toward the Sheriff's black GMC Tahoe. Several Sheriff's Department marked police cars rolled out of the parking lot and headed in different directions. The deputies would be setting up road blocks a few minutes before the breach.

Chapter Forty Nine

The Sheriff drove past the warehouse, turned off her lights and pulled into the parking lot for the auto body shop across the street. She pulled around behind the building and shut off the engine. Terry still had one deputy on surveillance inside the auto body shop and he unlocked the door as they approached.

Terry asked the deputy. "All quiet?"

"Yeah. Drivers started arriving a little bit ago and they have been firing up the semis and hooking up to the trailers. There is still one semi backed up to the loading dock. They closed the dock door about ten minutes ago, so I think they are done loading the last trailer."

Terry picked up the binoculars from the desk and looked out the window. The truck yard was lit up like the county fair. Not great for our side, he thought. One thing he saw that was a plus was that the electric gate was open, probably in anticipation of the trucks leaving. This was good for the SWAT guys.

"Snipers here yet?" Buck asked.

The deputy nodded. "Got here about an hour ago. They are on the roof."

The SWAT teams arrived at the building behind the warehouse, parked the cars and started moving quietly through the empty parking lot and up to the corner of the fence that the sneak and peek team had used for their entry. They had left the fence bolts loose, so it was just a matter of removing the nuts and slipping out the bolts. Quietly one by one, the DEA and the FBI SWAT teams passed through the opening in the fence and moved cautiously towards the back of the building. When they arrived at the back of the building each team headed for opposite ends of the building. The FBI team moved around the corner of the building and headed towards the front corner. They would hold at the corner until it was time to access the office.

The DEA team headed towards the back door. Once there, they assembled on each side of the door. The breacher attached a small wad of Semtex to the door knob and inserted the wireless fuse. He would set it off from his cell phone. They actually had an app for setting off explosives. Technology was amazing.

While those two teams got set in their respective positions, two FBI snipers found the roof access ladder for the building behind the warehouse and climbed to the roof. Once there, they moved to separate ends of the building, staying below the parapet as they ran. Once in position they sighted in their rifles and started their overwatch duties. These guys took their role in all this very seriously. They were responsible for all those other guys on the ground. They had a big job.

The Sheriff's SWAT team pulled to a stop at the corner, just down the street from the warehouse and shut off the lights on the assault vehicle. Once more each member of the team checked their gear and then checked the gear of the person next to them.

At this point all movement stopped. Everyone was in place. Terry Rubin began contacting each unit on his radio. The radios were all set to a special frequency that was reserved for only the highest law enforcement use. The SWAT team commanders on the ground and the snipers on the buildings responded with a single click over the microphone. Everyone was on radio silence.

He was just about to contact the deputies and the Durango police officers to set up the road blocks, when the first semi started roaring and pulled away from the fence at the far end of the yard, heading for the gate. Three additional semis pulled out right behind the first.

Terry picked up his radio. "All units, hold position, semis leaving the yard."

Terry, Buck and the Sheriff all breathed a sigh of relief when the trucks all turned the same way and headed toward 550. They were all worried that one might turn the opposite way and drive right past where the SWAT vehicle sat.

Terry gave the trucks five minutes to clear the area and then he radioed the Deputies and Durango PD to set the barriers. He then radioed Josh back in the conference room and asked him to contact the Colorado and New Mexico troopers and the tribal police and let them know which way the trucks were heading. He also reminded Josh to tell them not to intercept until they received word that the raid was in progress.

Terry checked his watch. It was now five minutes to six in the morning and the sun was just a slight pink swathe of color coming over the mountains. He looked at Buck and then the Sheriff. Each nodded. Terry picked up his radio.

"Team B. You are clear to access the office. Drivers are all inside."

One audio click.

"Team A. Time to roll."

One click.

Buck looked down the block and saw the SWAT assault vehicle turn the corner. Lights off and several figures hanging on either side of the vehicle.

At the same time, one of the team B members picked the front door lock, opened the door and six bodies entered the space. Two members remained at the corner of the building to keep an eye out.

Inside the office, four of the team members quickly and quietly cleared the space while the breacher placed a small wad of Semtex on the door knob, inserted the wireless fuse and the entire team moved down the wall and found cover.

A muffled voice came over the radio. "Team B, ready."

Terry picked up the radio. "Team C get ready to breach." Click.

The SWAT vehicle arrived at the entrance drive and turned in and moved towards the electric gate, which thankfully, still sat open. It started to move into position, ready to hit the roll up door.

Buck looked at Terry. He nodded.

Terry picked up the radio. "All teams, BREACH!"

Two simultaneous explosions could be heard at either end of the warehouse as the SWAT teams breached the two access doors. Immediately followed by the sound of four flash bangs going off. The SWAT assault vehicle roared up the ramp and hit the cargo door right dead center. The door flew in and landed on top of Blondy's rental car. The Swat vehicle hit the back of the car and drove it ten feet forward until it hit the fence and stopped.

Buck, Terry and the Sheriff threw open the front door of the auto body shop and ran towards the warehouse. Over the radio the various units were yelling. "Police, we have warrant!" "Federal Agents, everyone on the ground!" "Police, on the ground!"

"GUN!"

Terry, Buck and the Sheriff stopped short of the building as automatic weapons fire could be heard from several locations is the building.

"Drop the weapon!" From multiple voices. More shots fired.

Screams could be heard coming from inside.

"Man Down, Man Down!!"

"Runner, back door!" Multiple shouts.

Chapter Fifty

Moustache had just walked into the guard's office and Blondy was just walking out of the restroom when the first explosions rocked the building and the door to the main office blew into the warehouse and almost off its hinges. One of the guards had been standing right in front of the door when it blew and the door hit him square in the back and knocked him to the ground. He was down for the count. At the same time Blondy felt the concussion from the blast that took out the back door. He dove back into the restroom just as two flash bangs were thrown into the space and exploded simultaneously. The same thing happened as two more were thrown in from the main office.

The noise and smoke from the flash bangs had the desired effect and the kids started screaming and covering their eyes and ears as they fell to the floor. The space was soon flooded with people wearing all black and sporting ballistics vests and heavy weapons. Moustache was in the office and didn't get the full effect of the flash bang, but he still came out the door of the guard's office staggering and clawing at his ears. The rollup door suddenly came crashing down and almost hit him as it landed on the rental car. Even though he was having trouble seeing, Moustache raised his weapon and tried to aim at the people rushing around the smashed door.

"Police, we have a warrant!" "Federal agents, everyone on the ground!" "Police, on the ground!" "GUN!"

The first bullet hit Moustache in the chest. The next four followed suit and Moustache died before he hit the floor. Two of the other guards were able to recover enough from the flash bangs and even though they were having trouble standing and seeing, they managed to pull the triggers on their guns and spray bullets where they thought the intruders were located. Both men died in a hail of gun fire.

"Man Down, Man Down!"

Another guard came around the corner of the cages and raised his weapon.

"Drop the weapon!" The guard fired and was immediately put down by multiple rounds.

Blondy had a good idea who these guys were, and it puzzled him for a moment. "How did they know?" He had

been careful. Then he hit on it. "That
damn kid who tried to escape. He must
have thrown something over the fence.
Shit, Shit, Shit." He picked himself up
off the floor and cracked the restroom
door. It looked like the cops were all
inside the space, so he opened the door
and moved toward the back door.

He was almost to the door when he
heard a cop yell. "We have a runner."

Without looking back he ducked into
the cage and picked up one of the girls
who was lying on the floor crying and
holding her ears. He backed out of the
cage and immediately raised his gun and
placed the barrel against the back of her
head. Even though she could barely
stand, Blondy was able to crouch down
enough to stay behind her and not give
the approaching cops a shot. He
continued slowly backing up towards the
back door. He heard a chorus of voices,
"Drop your weapon!" and "Let the girl
go!" His hearing was finally clearing,
and he was able to see a little more
clearly. He reached the threshold of the
door and pinned himself and the girl
against the wall. Decision time.

Chapter Fifty One

Buck, Terry Rubin and Sheriff Sinclair, with guns drawn, entered through the glass door into the office and slowly stepped through the door into the warehouse. The inside of the warehouse looked like a war zone. The production tables they had seen on the camera were tipped over. Bodies were lying all over the floor, many crying and writhing in pain. Many had blood coming from their ears. To his left, Buck watched as one of the SWAT members was putting flex cuffs on the unconscious guard who had been hit by the door.

Buck headed towards the back of the building. As he approached the SWAT officers, he spotted Blondy pinned against the wall next to the back door holding a young girl in front of himself for protection. The officers were yelling for him to drop the weapon he held against her head and let the girl go. Buck stepped forward and was immediately grabbed by a SWAT officer.

He shrugged off his hand and looked at
Blondy.

"Sergeant Crank." He said. "Is
this how you want to go out? Protected
by a girl."

Buck held his gun at his side. The
room went silent. Weapons were lowered
as Buck was now in the line of fire.
Everyone froze.

Terry Rubin turned his back and
spoke quietly into his radio.
"Overwatch two, hostage situation. If
you have a shot, you have the green
light."

"Roger." Came the response.

Buck looked at Blondy. "You were
awarded a bronze star and a silver star
for bravery. I bet you didn't get them
by hiding behind a kid. Why don't you
let the girl go and drop the gun? You
don't need to die today."

Blondy looked up and Buck could see
instant recognition enter his eyes. The
cop from the parking lot shootout. What
are the odds. He also started to
calculate in his head his odds of staying
alive. He would either die in prison
from a lethal injection or from the shiv
of one of Carlos Rojas's paid killers.
He was screwed no matter what he did. He
made a decision.

Buck took another step forward and
stopped. He looked at Blondy and then he

saw it in Blondy's eyes.   Blondy had made his decision. Blondy started to slide step towards the door keeping the girl in front of him. Buck started to raise his pistol. Blondy's foot hit the threshold and he looked down at his foot. He glanced over his shoulder and saw two more SWAT cops pointing automatic weapons at him, from outside the building. He looked at Buck and smiled. Buck started to race forward. He was too late. Blondy stepped over the threshold and raised his head two inches over the girl's head. It was just enough. The sniper's bullet entered his skull between his left ear and his left eyebrow. The back of his skull blew out and splattered bone and brain matter over the wall behind him.

Buck caught the girl just as Blondy let her go. It was a completely involuntary movement because Blondy's life ended as soon as the bullet hit his brain. Blondy's body jerked to the right and slid down the wall, smearing more blood and brain as it went. Buck, holding the girl in one arm, holstered his pistol. It was all over.

Two SWAT officers walked up and took the girl out of Buck's arm. He looked down at Blondy. He stood for moment. Such a waste. He turned and walked back down the hall toward the warehouse. Several of the SWAT officers patted him on the back as he walked past. Buck simply nodded.

The scene in the warehouse was improving. Paramedics had arrived and were applying a pressure bandage to the left leg of one of the FBI SWAT guys. As it turned out, one of the guards, unable to see, had gotten off a lucky shot before he was hit with numerous bullets. Not so lucky for the SWAT member who was in the wrong place at the wrong time.

Paramedics were also working on some of the kids. It didn't look to Buck like their injuries were too severe. Some of them might suffer a little hearing loss, but they were alive and that was what mattered. Two of the kids had already been transported by ambulance. They were the most severely hurt, having gotten caught in the crossfire.

Terry spotted Buck and walked towards him. "What you tried to do back there was amazing."

Buck just nodded. He had mixed feelings about what had happened in the back hall and he would need to sort those out once he was alone.

Terry continued. "The troopers stopped all four trucks. One was headed for Salt Lake City, one was headed east on 160 toward Denver and two were headed south. The Ute Tribal Police stopped one just before it got to the state line and the New Mexico State Police stopped the other one just north of Farmington. FBI agents and the DEA guys out of Santa Fe

are already on their way to all four
stops. No one resisted."

Buck looked pleased. "What about
the other drivers here?"

"Two of them were catching a nap in
their rigs and three more were found safe
inside the little office. They will all
have headaches, but they are alive. Oh,
the guy with the moustache, Claire
Rinsgby had mentioned. He was the first
to die." Terry walked away to take a
call.

Sheriff Sinclair walked up. "All
in all, not a bad morning." Then she
looked around the warehouse. "Could have
been a lot worse. Not sure if we could
have done it without you. Unfortunately,
I am going to have the Feds in my county
for a long time trying to sort this all
out."

Buck smiled. "You got that right."
He stepped away from the Sheriff and
headed for the main office.

Inside the office, the SWAT guys
were taking pictures of each laptop as
they sat on the desks and then placing
them in evidence bags. They had already
grabbed the encrypted laptop. It had
been sitting in the little office in the
back. Buck nodded to the officers and
walked out the front door into the
morning air.

Buck sat on the front steps leading
to the office and looked out into the

parking lot. A crowd was starting to gather outside the yellow police tape that two deputies were putting up around the property. The first news trucks were arriving. He wondered if the Governor had alerted them. He just shook his head. That's when he noticed Jess Gonzales having a very animated phone call on the other side of the parking lot. She hung up the phone and spotted Buck sitting on the steps. She walked over.

Jess was out of breath and more excited than Buck had ever seen her. "Buck, this is huge. I was just on the phone with my director. If the amount of drugs we found in the one trailer is the same in all the others, this raid could be worth upwards of one hundred million dollars and that's conservative."

Buck looked at her, disbelieving. "Seriously. Holy shit! That would make this one of the biggest drug busts in history. Carlos Rojas is not going to be happy about this."

Jess laughed, as did Buck. "I need to run," she said. "We need to start inventorying all this stuff. The Director is flying in twenty more agents from other jurisdictions to help. See you later."

Terry Rubin found Buck a minute later. "I just spoke to Chief Chandler. They executed both warrants on Hector Vegas and on Dick Dillon's houses.

Everything went fine. Lots of tears and crying. I guess they scared the crap out of Hector's wife and kids when the used the battering ram on their front door. FBI is gathering evidence and Hector is in lock up at Durango PD."

Buck stood up and held out his hand. "You did an awesome job on this Terry. First class police work." Terry shook Buck's hand.

Terry just stood there speechless. Buck let go of Terry's hand and said. "I will catch up with you later. Time to make some calls. If this thing is as big as Jess thinks it is, the Governor is gonna want to be involved." Buck stepped away from Terry and pulled out his phone.

Chapter Fifty Two

The Director answered on the first ring. "Is it over?"

"Yes sir. And it is going to be a whole lot bigger than any of us expected. This could potentially be the biggest drug bust in history." He proceeded to fill in the Director on all the details.

When Buck finished, there was a moment of silence on the other end of the phone. Then the Director said, "OK Buck. I am going to call the Governor and fill him in. Max Clinton and the mobile crime lab should be there in a couple hours. I will let the Governor know that you would prefer to stay in the background and let the locals get all the credit. Awesome job Buck. Please let everyone on the team know I said so. OK?"

"Yes sir. That will be fine. And thank you sir. I am going to stay here for a couple more days to help wrap up what I can and then I am heading home. If you need me, that's where I will be." Buck disconnected the call.

The next couple hours were a blur as Buck and Terry Rubin continued to coordinate the work going on in the field. Max Clinton arrived a little after noon, with her forensics team and the CBI mobile crime lab. Her arrival was followed within minutes by the FBI forensics team, out of Denver, and their mobile crime lab. Max immediately introduced herself to the FBI's lead forensic analyst and they began coordinating the work of gathering evidence. There would be plenty of work to go around.

A couple hours after the raid on the warehouse, the trucks that had left the yard early, began to arrive back at the warehouse. It was decided by all concerned, that it would be easier to have the trucks escorted back to Durango so that all the evidence could be processed in one location and the contents of the trucks could be properly inventoried and documented.

While the first two trucks that returned were opened, Buck noted the arrival of Robert Townsend, Special Agent in Charge of the Denver office of ICE, Immigration and Customs Enforcement, and several car loads of ICE agents. Buck walked over to greet Townsend. They talked for a few minutes about the shootout and exchanged pleasantries. Buck then informed Townsend that there were still a couple of the kids on site. They were being held in the office area and were being interviewed by a couple Spanish speaking deputies. Each young person, except those that had been transported to the hospital, were photographed, fingerprinted and were advised of their Miranda rights. Since there were so many people on site inside the warehouse, it needed to be determined what role each person played, before they were released and transported to the Sheriff's office where they would be held until ICE could take them into custody. They were also being evaluated as to their medical conditions. Many were already starting to show signs of opioid withdrawal.

Townsend informed Buck that he would send his team over to the Sheriff's office to start processing the kids. He told Buck they would be transported, as soon as they were medically released, to a holding facility in Alamosa and that deportation proceeding would start immediately. Buck thanked Townsend for his help and walked back to the two trailers that were being inventoried.

Hank Clancy, FBI, pulled into the truck yard followed by three more black, government issue SUV's containing a dozen more agents on loan from several different field offices. He spotted Buck and waved. The remaining two trucks arrived at the same time, escorted by Colorado State Troopers and two Southern Ute Tribal Police units. The trailers were backed up to the loading dock. Jess met Buck and Hank Clancy at the back of one of the trailers. The FBI videographer started documenting the scene as Jess had one of her agents cut the lock on the trailer with a pair of bolt cutters. As the videographer had done twice before, he carefully documented the lock being cut and being removed from the hasp.

Two DEA agents then cleared the hasps and swung open the doors. Everyone stared at what they saw, some hardly believing their eyes. Inside the trailer were crates marked as containing AR type assault rifles. When the inventory was completed, in the next couple days, it would be determined that there were two hundred such crates with each crate containing six brand new rifles. The inventory would also reveal over four hundred handguns of varying calibers and almost a half million rounds of ammunition. Enough fire power to arm a small army. It looked like Carlos Rojas was preparing for war.

However, the biggest surprise was what sat strapped down in the middle of the trailer. Most of the observers had never seen that much money in one place. The money had been shrink wrapped together to make a solid block four feet long, four feet wide and almost six feet tall. Buck and Jess both let out a whistle. Hank stood speechless. Terry Rubin had just arrived on the dock with the Southern Ute Police Chief and the officer who had made the initial stop of this particular trailer. They were all having trouble understanding what they were looking at.

The Ute Police Chief was the first person to speak. "Holy Cow."

Buck looked at him and responded. "You can say that again."

Jess Gonzales, DEA, smiled. "There are millions of dollars there. Man did we put the hurt on the Sonoma Cartel."

Everyone started to come out of their stupor. Hank Clancy immediately phoned his SWAT Commander, who was somewhere in the warehouse, to have one of his men bring around the FBI SWAT vehicle, which was fully armored and secure and to have several of his SWAT officer assemble at the trailer. He directed his commander to disconnect the semi from the trailer and park the SWAT vehicle in front of the trailer. He then ordered the trailer doors closed and he assigned four SWAT agents to stand guard over the trailer. He needed some time to figure out what to do with all that money.

Buck had stepped away from the group and immediately placed a call to Gerald Choo. Gerald Choo was the Agent in Charge of the Denver office of Alcohol, Tobacco and Firearms. The ATF would take possession of the weapons from the trailer, inventory everything and

then open an investigation to determine
the origin of the weapons. When Gerald
answered his phone Buck said, "Jerry,
have I got a deal for you."

        Buck went on to tell him about the
raid and the trailer full of weapons they
had just opened. After a few minutes of
conversation, Gerald told Buck that he
would have a team on the ground inside of
two hours to take possession of the
weapons and start investigating how the
cartel was able to lay their hands on
that many weapons. Choo told Buck that
he was not aware of any large arms thefts
recently or any missing weapons from any
military weapons depots. Choo thanked
Buck and hung up.

        Buck had gotten several texts and
calls from his kids, but he didn't have
time to talk so he sent them a group text
to let them know he was OK and he would
talk to them later.

Chapter Fifty Three

The area around the truck garage had taken on almost a carnival atmosphere. In spite of the fact that the streets surrounding the warehouse had been cordoned off and no one was allowed near the warehouse. The streets outside the barricades were filled with people from all over the county. Many of the business parking lots surrounding the blocked streets were filled with various types of media vehicles and Buck was amazed to see that in just a short period of time, even the major national networks had arrived on the scene. He wondered to himself, again, if maybe the Governor had something to do with the large turn out

Buck was a familiar face to many of the local and statewide reporters, so he tried to stay back from their view. Even so, several times he had heard someone call out his name and shout out a question or two. Several reporters, who had his cell phone number, tried to call. He ignored them all. He was not interested in being part of the story.

The Sheriff had called Jimmy Palumbo to see if he could arrange to get food and drinks sent over to the warehouse. By this time in the day, everyone was running on empty and she hoped some food might help. Jimmy had jumped on the phone and started calling his network of restaurant contacts and charity groups he worked with and within two hours several Durango police officers were rolling into the lot, their patrol cars filled with food and drinks for all.

Buck grabbed a sub sandwich that had been donated by a local shop and a cold bottle of Coke and found a shady spot on the street side of the parking lot. He sat under a tree and devoured his sandwich. July in the mountains still got hot and everyone appreciated the break. Buck looked around the parking lot of the warehouse. There wasn't a parking spot to be had and he doubted they could fit many more people in the lot.

Buck leaned back against the trunk of the tree and within minutes found himself nodding off. He was almost asleep when he snapped out of it and decided he needed to keep moving. That's when he noticed Jess Gonzales, DEA, and Hank Clancy, FBI, heading his way. They each had a sandwich and a bottle of something cold.

"Mind if we join you?" asked Hank

"Pull up a piece of shade. You two look as beat as I feel."

They both sat down in Buck's shady spot and went to town on their sandwiches. As they ate, Jess filled Buck in on what had taken place in the last hour or two. She told him that the drivers' paperwork had proved to be a treasure trove of information. Jess had collected all the destination and delivery information from each of the semis and had forwarded the information to her boss in Washington. The information proved invaluable. Her office had the locations of eight smaller local distribution centers that had been set up by the cartel in eight major western and southwestern cities.

The DEA office in Washington, in conjunction with the FBI and local law enforcement in each of those cities, had used the information from the raid this morning to get search warrants for all eight locations. As of an hour ago, raids had been mounted and were now taking place at each location. Several of the locations raided so far did contain small amounts of drugs, mostly local stuff the cartel had been able to get their hands on while they waited for the big shipments coming from Durango, but they also netted eight more encrypted laptops, which were being bagged up and would soon be headed to the NSA.

Buck said. "That's awesome Jess. Sounds like we really hit Carlos Rojas where it hurts."

Jess smiled and was just about to answer when Buck's phone rang. He checked the number and answered the call.

"Yes sir", said Buck. The Director was calling to fill Buck in on the cartel attorney they were staking out last night and this morning. Buck listened intently and hung up the phone. He filled Jess and Hank in on what the Director had just told him.

It seems the attorney was not hiding from anyone. He hadn't been seen at his residence or his office because he had taken his wife to dinner at a fancy downtown Denver restaurant to celebrate their anniversary and had gotten a room at a hotel for the night. He was unaware he was under surveillance until he turned on the Sunday morning news and saw a developing story about the raid in Durango. The lawyer and his wife quickly dressed, had the valet bring their car around and raced home to get their two kids and their pre-packed emergency suit cases.

The attorney was a smart guy and he circled the blocks around their house several times to see if it was being watched. Not seeing any one in the neighborhood who didn't belong, he pulled into the driveway, ran into the house, grabbed the kids and their "Go" bags and headed for the car.

While he was grabbing everything they would need to travel, his wife was paying the babysitter and scooting her out the door. They all jumped into the car and he pulled out of the driveway and headed for Centennial Airport. First, they had to pass back through the security gate at the entrance to the neighborhood. The attorney lived in a gated community.

On the way home, his wife had called the charter jet company he already had an account with and arranged for an immediate flight to Cabo San Lucas, where they had a beautiful town house that looked out over the ocean. The charter service always kept pilots on standby for their more discerning clients and she was told that the pilots would be at the airport within half an hour.

CBI agents Tracy and Doonen had found a real nice place to park their car just inside the entrance to the golf course across the street from the attorney's gated community. They had been able to park in the very first parking space, which gave them a great view of the main gate and they had spotted the attorney's car as soon as it entered the drive way and stopped at the security gate. There were only two ways to get in and out of the community. Through the main entrance or through a

rear service entrance. Tracy and Doonen
had asked the Arapahoe County Sheriff to
have a deputy posted across the street
from the service entrance. They called
him to let him know the attorney had come
home.

The Attorney exited through the
main entrance and headed south on
University Blvd. He eventually turned at
Arapahoe Road and headed east. Tracy and
Doonen were four cars back at the light.
The Arapahoe County deputy was two cars
behind them. The little parade proceeded
east on Arapahoe Road until the attorney
turned right at the sign for Centennial
Airport. Two blocks up, he turned right,
into the parking lot for Centennial
Charters. Tracy lit up her flashers and
hit the siren. The attorney hit the gas,
drove around the parking lot and was
stopped dead in his tracks by four
Arapahoe County Sheriff's cars. The
deputies were out of their cars with guns
drawn. Tracy pulled up behind him.
While Tracy held her position at the back
of the car, Doonen, with gun drawn,
approached the driver's door. She
ordered the attorney and his wife out of
the car while two deputies positioned
themselves to either side of the
passenger door.

The arrest of the attorney and his
wife continued without incident and they
were booked into the Arapahoe County
Sheriff's jail. The attorney immediate
requested a meeting with the US Attorney

for Colorado. The US Attorney, Ernesto
Salvatore, and his attorney were now
sitting in a conference room negotiating
a spot in the Witness Protection Program,
in exchange for everything he knew about
the Sonoma Cartel. Additional CBI agents
and Arapahoe County Deputies along with a
couple FBI agents from Denver were now
executing a search warrant on the
attorney's house. His neighbors stood on
their lawns and looked stunned that this
was happening in their little private
paradise.

Chapter Fifty Four

Doctor Kramer, the county's Forensic Pathologist, was just walking out of the warehouse as Buck was crossing the parking lot. Buck looked up to see the Doctor standing on the loading dock.

"Hey Doc. You doing OK?" The Doctor looked as tired as everyone else.

"I'll say one thing Agent Taylor. Things sure get interesting when you're around." The Doctor smiled. "Haven't been this busy in years."

The Doctor had spent most of the day examining the remains of the deceased guards. He had just finished with the last body, the one by the back door, and had given the all clear for the paramedics and ambulance crews to start removing the bodies from the scene and taking them to the autopsy suite at the Sheriff's office. He was going to run out of refrigerator room and was trying to find some additional storage. He told Buck that he had requested help from Montrose County and Grand Junction and that two more certified Forensic Pathologists would be onsite first thing in the morning to assist with the autopsies. This was going to be a busy couple of days.

He looked at Buck and Buck noticed the sadness in his eyes. "What a damn shame. And for what? Those young folks are going to go through hell until they get the opioids out of their systems and then they will have to face the reality of what they had been put through. Some of them may never recover. Such a shame." He nodded to Buck and headed for his car.

Buck made a slow pass though the warehouse stopping now and then to talk to one of the evidence techs. As he passed by the small office, he stopped to watch the paramedics placing Moustache into the body bag. He thought to himself. "I wonder if we will ever find out who this guy was?"

He walked towards the back door where one of the ambulance crews was just wheeling in the gurney. He stopped and looked at Blondy. He was no longer propped up against the wall. Dr. Kramer had laid him down to conduct his field examination. Buck looked at the bloody streak on the wall. He had to agree with the doctor. What a waste. Buck thought back to the moment Blondy raised his head up. Buck had seen the smile and he knew that Blondy had chosen the best way out.

He knew when he raised up his head that his life was already forfeit. Carlos Rojas would never allow this betrayal and failure to go unpunished.

Buck found Terry Rubin sitting in the small office. He was just sitting there staring at the wall. Terry was bone weary and he had every right to be. Buck gave Terry a little salute with his right hand and turned and headed for the door. For the most part, his job was finished. This investigation had moved into other states and had now become mostly a federal affair. He would now be on the periphery and that would be fine with him.

The Sheriff left the warehouse several hours earlier and had taken Buck's tactical gear with her. Buck stood outside the warehouse. It was a beautiful night and he decided to walk the half mile back to the Sheriff's office. He unclipped his badge from his belt and put it in his pocket and untucked his shirt to cover his gun. He headed toward the deputy who was manning the entrance to the crime scene, signed himself out and started walking. He wasn't in a big hurry to get anywhere. He was also glad to see that most of the people who had surrounded the warehouse earlier had left and no one noticed him walk away.

As Buck entered the parking lot for the Sheriff's Department, he saw that several of the news trucks were now parked in the lot and the Sheriff and Durango Police Chief Chandler were standing in front of the building and were speaking to the media. Much of the crowd of onlookers from the warehouse were also present. The Sheriff was explaining the events of the day and wanted to assure all the citizens of the city and the county that the situation was under control and there was no further danger. She also explained that there was still a lot of evidence to examine and that there would be a press conference early the next morning and the FBI and DEA would be available to answer questions.

One of the reporters, Buck recognized from one of the Denver TV Stations, asked about the shootout that had happened in the hotel parking lot the night before. Chief Chandler explained that the events of the night before were not related, at all, to the drug raid today. He went on to explain that an agent with the Colorado Bureau of Investigation had been ambushed in the parking lot by two individuals, who later were identified as prime suspects in a triple homicide in Teller County.

The CBI agent was in Durango following up on a lead and had no idea the two suspects had followed him from Teller County. He explained that both individuals had died at the scene from multiple gunshots and that the CBI agent

had been uninjured. He further explained
that his office and the Sheriff's office
had conducted a thorough investigation
and determined the Agent's use of deadly
force was justified. Due to the nature
of the Agent's work, he would not be
identified at this time.

Chief Chandler concluded by telling
the reporters that they would need to
contact the Teller County Sheriff's
Department or the Colorado Bureau of
Investigations for more information.

The press conference continued, but
Buck was done. He entered the side door
and headed up the stairs to the
conference room. He was hoping to say
goodbye to the FBI sneak and peek team
but when he stepped into the conference
room, the space was empty. They had
already packed up their gear and were
probably headed back to Denver. They
were good people and he was grateful for
their help. He would make sure to let
Hank Clancy know how much they had helped
this investigation.

Chapter Fifty Five

The young folks who had been cleared by ICE agents were being held in the public meeting hall that was attached to the Sheriff's Office. Many of them were asleep on the floor while others sat shaking in chairs. Opioid withdrawal had taken hold of many of the kids and Buck felt sorry for them. They had been through so much already and now this. Buck spotted Robert Townsend, the ICE Agent in Charge and walked over to him.

"Hey Bob. How are they doing?"

Townsend, who had just hung up his phone, turned to Buck. "Some of them are doing OK right now. The doctors at the hospital said we need to get them to a holding facility as soon as we can. The withdrawals will only get worse." Townsend hesitated for a moment.

Buck said, "What?"

"We don't really have the facilities to take care of illegals going through opioid withdrawal, especially this many. I have been calling everyone I know for ideas and I have a lot of people working on this, but this is way beyond anything we have ever dealt with.

"Perhaps I can help with that?" The voice came from the main doors leading to the public meeting room and both Buck and Townsend looked towards the voice.

Sandi Calhoun, Attorney at Law, stood in the doorway holding what looked to Buck like a legal document. Buck had never met Sandi and his first and only contact with her had occurred just the other day when they spoke on the phone. Buck had been in the audience at the National Police Chiefs Conference in Denver this past April when Sandi Calhoun had given the opening night keynote speech. The subject of her speech was human trafficking and Buck had been very impressed with what he heard.

Sandi Calhoun had been born and raised Catholic in a primarily Hispanic neighborhood in West Denver. Divorced early in her marriage, she found herself as a single mother left to raise her three young sons on her own. At the same time she was struggling to raise her sons she was also putting herself though school. First at the University of Colorado in Boulder and then at the University of Denver Law school, where she graduated at the top of her class. Sandi had initially gone to work for a large Denver law firm, but she never found satisfaction in the job. Her passion was to help those less fortunate, so she finally left the huge firm and put up her shingle above the door of a rundown little storefront in Five Points, a mostly downtrodden neighborhood just north of Downtown Denver.

Over the years her practice outgrew the little storefront and she moved her firm to a larger building a few blocks away from the original location, but she kept the original storefront location. She staffed it with new, young attorneys who wanted to change the world. The old storefront would keep them closer to the people she had grown to love.

Sandi's practice originally started out handling immigration cases and cases involving people who were being stepped on by the system, and by life. A lot of her work involved pro bono cases and many of her clients, when they could, paid with food and things they had made. No one was ever turned away because they couldn't pay. To make ends meet and pay her staff, she also had attorneys working for her who handled typical legal cases, DUI's, contracts, mergers and acquisitions, personal injury and some small criminal matters. For Sandi, though, it was the helpless and the hopeless that got her full attention.

Over the years, Sandi had become the go to lawyer in Denver for those seeking asylum in the United States. She never shied away from a controversial case and she became a familiar face on the nightly news, always fighting for the rights of the oppressed. She never cared about her clients ethnic or religious backgrounds. If you were oppressed or lived in fear of going back to your original country, Sandi was the person you wanted in your corner.

Sandi was a powerful force to be reckoned with and as the years progressed, she found herself being invited to speak at rallies for various causes all around the state. She became a vocal activist for many causes, but she still focused mostly on causes that dealt with human and sex trafficking. She was on the Board of Directors of several charitable foundations. She also became a leading expert on human trafficking and was in high demand as a speaker and as a guest lecturer at law schools all around the country.

Five years before Buck had heard Sandi speak at the Police Chiefs Conference, she was diagnosed with Metastatic Breast Cancer. The breast cancer had been found during a routine mammogram and additional scans had found that the cancer had also spread to her spine. Sandi was devastated. She did not accept the fact that her life could be over. There was too much left to do and too many people who depended on her, especially her three sons. Sandi's life

was about to be turned upside down, but
she vowed to fight the cancer with
everything she had. She had faced many
powerful adversaries in court and this
would become the biggest fight of her
life. Her faith in her doctors was
strong, but her faith in God was an even
more powerful force in her life. She
would fight hard, but she would also pray
to God for help. Her support network of
family and friends was huge, and she felt
their love and support every step of the
way. Sandi had set goals for herself as
she battled this dreaded disease, but the
most important goal would be the one that
would stay with her through the entire
fight. She would live to dance with
each one of her sons at their weddings
and that became her focus.

So far, Sandi Calhoun was winning
the battle. She fought like a trooper
through the double mastectomy, the
numerous chemo treatments and the
reconstruction. The cancer in her spine
had completely disappeared and she
thanked God every day for that incredible
miracle. Her ongoing scans had shown no
new cancer over the past three years.
Sandi believed that God had chosen her
for a mission and she would not let him
down. Her passion for the less fortunate
amongst us continued to grow and was now
stronger than ever. She would move
heaven and earth to help those in need.

All that love, support and her
incredible faith in God had paid off.

During the past year and a half, Sandi
had danced with two of her sons at their
weddings. She had one more wedding to
go. She had also been at the hospital
for the birth of her first grandchild.
Something she never thought might happen.
She felt truly blessed and fortunate.
Now her attention would turn towards
helping the young people from the
warehouse.

Chapter Fifty Six

Sandi Calhoun was an attractive Latina with shoulder length brown hair and a smile that lit up the room. But the first thing Buck noticed were her eyes. Buck had never seen eyes that were so expressive. Just looking at them and you could feel the passion she had for her job and the compassion she felt for her clients. Sandi Calhoun's presence filled the room. She was smart, soft-spoken and charming. Buck had dealt with a lot of attorneys over the years and he knew one thing immediately. Sandi Calhoun was good at her job because people who met her instantly liked her.

She reminded Buck a little of his late wife. Lucy was the social butterfly in their family and just like Sandi, here in this moment, Lucy's presence had filled any room she entered. Buck missed her terribly.

Sandi wore an impeccably tailored light grey business suit, grey suede shoes that matched the color of her suit perfectly and a burgundy blouse that was cut a few inches below her neck. Around her neck she wore a small silver cross on a very fine silver chain. She walked into the room and reached out her hand.

"Agent Townsend, it is nice to see you again." Bob Townsend shook her hand.

"Good evening Counselor", he said. "What brings you here?"

She turned toward Buck and extended her hand. "Sandi Calhoun, Attorney at Law, and you would be?"

Buck shook her hand. "Buck Taylor, Ma'am. Colorado Bureau of Investigation, nice to meet you." Buck noticed that she gave him a very slight wink with her right eye. She turned back to Townsend.

"Agent Townsend. I am going to make your day." She handed him the paper she was carrying. "What you have there is a Cease and Desist Order signed by US District Court Judge Henry Morales ordering you to stop all contact with the individuals involved in this case and to stop any deportation proceedings you have either already started or will start in the immediate future. It further orders you to place all those individuals under my custody effective immediately."

Bob Townsend read the order in full. Buck could have sworn he almost saw the typically stoic agent in charge smile an almost imperceptible smile.

Townsend stopped reading the order and lowered the paper.

"Ms. Calhoun. How did you get involved in this and how did you get this order so quickly? The raid only happened this morning and the press didn't even have the story until much later. You have a source in this investigation?"

Sandi smiled. "You know I can't discuss that with you, Agent Townsend. Attorney client privilege. Now if you have a problem with this order, we can certainly give Judge Morales a call at home. I'm sure he wouldn't have any problem explaining this order to you, this late on a Sunday night. Shall we give him a call? I have his home number right here." She held up her phone.

Townsend really wanted to act like he was in charge, but this was one fight he was definitely going to lose. Judge Morales was a real hard ass when it came to protecting the rights of undocumented individuals and the last thing he needed today was a judge chewing on his ass. Buck had to turn his head and make believe he was checking his phone for messages, so he could silently chuckle to himself. Sandi Calhoun was good. Very good.

Buck turned back and broke the silence. "Ms. Calhoun, do you have a plan in place to take care of all these kids? They will all need special care due to the opioid addiction and they have

all been tortured and some of the girls
have been sexually abused for most likely
a fairly long period of time."

Buck looked around the room at the
kids. What they were going through and
were about to go through broke his heart.
Townsend nodded his head in agreement.
He was glad Buck had asked the question.

"We certainly do Agent Taylor."
Sandi responded.

Sandi went on to explain that she
had made arrangements with several
medical transportation companies to head
down to Durango to pick up the young
people who had been cleared by the police
and were medically able to be moved.
Most would be taken by ambulance. The
kids who were hardest hit with withdrawal
symptoms would be transported by air.
They would all be under constant medical
supervision until they reached one of
three drug rehabilitation facilities she
had arrangements with in Denver. Those
facilities had agreed to donate their
services and would supervise the kids as
they went through the withdrawal
protocols.

She also had several doctors and
nurses who were willing to volunteer
their services to make sure all the
medical needs of the kids were met. She
assured Townsend that all three
facilities were top tier, secure
facilities and that the kids would not be
allowed to leave the facility without

supervision. While they were receiving treatment, her office would make them available to the authorities for any interviews that might be needed in the preparation of the case against the people who had perpetrated this heinous crime. Each young person would be represented by an attorney from her office or another volunteer attorney and the attorney would be present at all interviews.

Once the kids were medically cleared by the doctors and if the authorities no longer needed the kids to be available for legal proceedings, the kids would be given two choices. They could choose to return to Mexico, knowing full well that their lives might be in considerable jeopardy from the cartel or they could choose to seek asylum in the United States. If they chose the latter, lawyers from Sandi's office or other volunteer lawyers would file all the necessary paperwork needed to request asylum. Those who chose to return to Mexico would be sent home by plane, as soon as they were able to travel, to the closest major airport to their final destination. They would not have to go through deportation proceedings.

Bob Townsend knew he should ask questions or object to something, but this late in the evening he was tired and ready for this day to be over. The plan as outlined was sound and deep down inside he was grateful that someone was

taking this out of his hands. He knew he
would sleep easier tonight knowing these
kids were in good hands.

He looked at Sandi. "Sounds like
you have done your homework on this. I
don't see any reason to bother Judge
Morales this late. I will forward a copy
of this order to my office in Washington
and let them know about the arrangements
you have made. I doubt anyone will have
any issues."

Buck couldn't agree more. For ICE
and the Border Patrol, this was going to
be a public relations nightmare. A lot
of powerful people in Washington were
going to be asking a lot of hard
questions in the next few weeks to find
out how thirty some drugged kids had been
snuck across the border. One of the
biggest battle the newly elected
President had been waging was a huge
effort to make our borders more secure.
This was going to cut deep.

Sandi smiled. "Thank you, Agent
Townsend. Now if you have another minute
we should step outside and make sure we
have all the documents you will need to
release these kids into my custody. The
medical transports should start arriving
in a couple hours."

Buck decided it was time to head
back to his hotel. He shook hands all
around and told Sandi Calhoun that it had
been a pleasure meeting her. He wished

them both a good night and walked out
into the cool night air.

Chapter Fifty Seven

The incessant ringing of a phone woke Buck from a really deep sleep. It took him a second to realize where he was and he almost fell out of bed as he reached for the phone. He had crashed hard last night when he got back to his hotel room and was asleep as soon as his head hit the pillow.

He looked at the screen, but he was having trouble focusing so he just hit the green button.

"Taylor!" Buck said in a voice that sounded a little too loud.

Director Jackson was on the other end of the call. "Wake the hell up Buck. The Governor is holding a press conference at the warehouse in little over an hour and he wants you there."

Buck tried valiantly to get his brain to engage. "Sorry Director. Didn't realize it was you. Please repeat that."

Speaking more slowly this time, almost exaggerating each word, the Director replied. "OK Buck. I am in Durango with the Governor. We arrived a little bit ago. The Governor is going to hold a press conference at the warehouse in just about an hour. He wants you there."

Buck finally focused. "Yes Sir. Got it. I am on my way."

The Director hung up.

Buck grabbed a quick shower, found a clean T-shirt in the pile on the floor and put it on. He clipped his badge and gun to his belt and headed for the car. He wasn't surprised that the Governor would be in town. This case was huge and the Governor would get all the political mileage out of this that he could. This bust would go a long way to appeasing the law and order crowd who typically had nothing good to say about the liberal Governor. Not that Governor Richard J Kennedy cared much about what most people thought. He had won the election for Governor, little over a year ago, by one of the largest margins in the history of the Colorado Governor's race. Regular people loved him.

Buck had to park on the street leading to the warehouse. There was no way to get near the place with the crowds of people and the massive amount of news trucks. Buck was amazed. The news media's presence had grown huge since he left the site last night. He even spotted news vans from several international stations and quite a few from Mexico. He wondered how a news conference like this was going to go over in the house of Carlos Rojas, the leader of the Sonoma Cartel. He had a feeling people down there were going to die. Carlos Rojas had a bad temper on a short fuse.

The Governor was setting up for a hell of a show. The money trailer had been pulled into the middle of the yard and the doors were wide open. Inside stood some very unhappy looking FBI SWAT guys, wearing full tactical gear and covering their faces with black balaclavas. Standing off to the side of the trailer, Hank Clancy, FBI, was in a somewhat heated discussion with Kevin Jackson, the Director of the Colorado Bureau of Investigation. Hank looked as unhappy as his SWAT guys. Director Jackson was pointing his hand at the Governor and was obviously trying to make a point. Hank didn't look like he was buying whatever the Director was selling. DEA agents, Colorado State Troopers and Sheriff's deputies surrounded the trailer. All of them were armed with assault rifles.

All the doors to the warehouse were closed. Inside, the forensic teams were still collecting evidence and processing the scene, the DEA was sorting and cataloguing the drugs and the ATF was inventorying all the weapons that had been seized. There was still a ton of work to be done and it would be another very long day for everyone involved.

The huge block of money had been pulled forward, so it sat right in the open doorway of the trailer. A lower platform had been erected in front of the trailer, so the Governor would be standing slightly below the block of money. This would make for some great pictures. The Governor was in his element. Governor Richard J Kennedy was a multi-millionaire business man and a seasoned politician, having spent 20 years in the Colorado legislature before running for Governor. For most public appearances the Governor was usually seen in a stylish three-piece suit. Today he was dressed for the people. Governor Kennedy was wearing jeans, western boots and a denim shirt, open at the neck with his sleeves were rolled up. The Governor was extremely fit for a gentleman of seventy years old and Buck thought he looked good standing up there with all that money.

The Governor stepped up on the stage, followed by a decent size contingent of folks representing the various agencies that had been involved in the raid. Standing to both sides of the stage and positioned so as not to block the Governor and the big block of money, the Governor introduce his partners. Everyone was represented.

FBI, DEA, Sheriff's office, Durango Police Department, ATF, ICE, Colorado and New Mexico State police and the Southern Ute Tribal Police. CBI Director Jackson stood right next to the Governor.

The Governor started out by saying how thrilled he was to be back in Durango, a part of the state he really loved. He thanked the news media for coming to cover this press conference. He then proceeded to explain the events of the past twenty-four hours. Hank Clancy, FBI, had given the Governor's Aide a detailed but relatively vague outline to follow. There were still elements of this investigation that Hank wanted to keep out of the media. For the most part the Governor followed the outline as he spoke. He of course, mentioned the huge block of money, as the cameras all around him started clicking once again. He told the press that although they were still counting, the Treasury Department estimated that the block of money could contain as much as a hundred million dollars.

He told them that it was estimated by the DEA that the street value of the drugs seized here in Colorado and at the eight other smaller distribution sites was estimated to be over two hundred and fifty million dollars. Buck thought that estimate might be a little high, but the Governor was having fun with the facts and he had the press eating out of his hand.

So far, the investigation had resulted in at least fifty arrests directly related to the crime and the investigation would possibly yield as many as two hundred arrests by the time it was completed. He verified that five suspected cartel members had been killed during the raid, that one FBI SWAT officer had been injured and that two of the thirty-four kids that were being held as slaves, were in the hospital having been caught in the crossfire during the raid. One of the kids was clinging to life and had been airlifted to Denver for surgery to remove a bullet near her spine and the other was still in Durango and was now listed in stable condition.

The Governor told those assembled that this would go down in history as one of the largest drug raids ever conducted in the United States and that they were expecting the prosecution of those responsible to go on for years. He didn't mention Carolos Rojas by name, but he did say that they felt that this was a huge blow to the suspected growth of the Sonoma Cartel, north of the border. He then spent a long time praising all those involved and thanking them all for their efforts.

Governor Kennedy was never afraid to be shown up by anyone and he was more than willing to share the spotlight. For the next hour, the Governor answered questions and as much as possible, pushed those questions over to the rest of the

folks onstage with him. Buck felt the
news media was getting a pretty good
picture of what had transpired, and he
was pleased that the Governor had given
credit where credit was due. He was also
glad the Governor hadn't dragged him into
this circus.

Chapter Fifty Eight

Buck was standing just off to the side of the trailer, talking with Max Clinton, the head of the state crime lab, when the press conference broke up. The Governor spotted him and made a beeline straight for him. Grabbing Buck's hand, the Governor said,

"Buck, you guys did a great job here. Excellent police work. I've already personally thanked the Sheriff and her team. I am very proud of the way they handled this. I will make sure to thank everyone I haven't thanked so far, before I leave. I also wanted to tell you that I am very pleased you were not injured during the shootout. What a crazy thing to happen in the middle of an investigation like this. Wow."

The Governor was ecstatic. Buck thanked him and told him he was glad he survived as well. Director Jackson came up and shook Buck's hand. The Governor's Aide also walked up and told the Governor that they needed to leave soon. They had other appointments in Denver that they needed to get to.

The Governor shook Buck's hand again. He leaned in a little closer and said.

"I understand that all those kids are going to be turned over to Sandi Calhoun and she has arranged to get them the help they need. I am so glad ICE was able to work things out with Ms. Calhoun. I wonder how she was able to get that order from Henry so quickly." Then he smiled at Buck and walked away.

There was no doubt in Buck's mind that the Governor had probably had a lot to do with Sandi Calhoun getting that cease and desist order. He was well aware that the Governor and Judge Henry Morales had attended the same law school and were brothers in the same fraternity.

Director Jackson smiled as the Governor walked away.

"He's a sly old fox, ain't he?"

Buck nodded in agreement and the Director laughed. "When you feel you are wrapped up here head home for a break. I'll call you in a couple days." The Director walked off after the Governor.

Buck spotted Hank Clancy and Jess Gonzales talking to the FBI SWAT Commander. The rest of the SWAT team was in the process of locking up the trailer and breathing a sigh of relief that they

could now get that money out of here.
Buck had noticed that all the crates of
weapons had been removed from the
trailer.

Buck asked Hank if they had come up
with a way to get all that money
someplace safe, so they could count it.
Hank told him the plan. It was decided by
people a lot higher up the food chain
than Hank, that the best way to transport
the money was exactly like the cartel had
intended. They would leave the money in
the trailer. As soon as the press was
clear of the truck yard two semis would
leave the yard an hour apart. Each semi
would be part of a convoy of SWAT teams,
State Troopers, FBI and DEA agents. The
State Patrol would also provide air
support over each group. Having a decoy
semi and a huge convoy of cops should
stop anybody from trying to ambush the
convoys. Their destination would be the
Federal Reserve Building in Denver. They
had the equipment to count huge
quantities of money and the means to
safely store it.

Buck told Hank that he thought the
plan was probably the best option, then
he took Jess by the arm and walked
towards the warehouse.

"You doing OK?" He asked her.

"Nothing a little sleep won't
cure", she responded.

"Good", said Buck. "I just wanted you to know that I owe you and if you ever need anything, all you have to do is call."

"That's not necessary, Buck. We are friends and friends always have each others backs." She gave him a big hug. Buck held her tight for a minute.

"I heard a rumor that there might be a Deputy Directors job in your future." Buck said.

Jess backed away and looked at him. "How do you do that? Is there anything you are not plugged into?"

Buck held up his hands in surrender. "Hey, what can I tell you? I'm a detective. Comes with the job."

Jess just smiled and headed back to her team. Hank was getting all the various agencies set up for the drive back to Denver. At this point two identical trailers attached to identical semis were facing the road. Everyone was taking their places.

Sheriff Sinclair walked up and stood next to Buck. She had dressed in her class "A" uniform for the press conference. She looked sharp. She also looked as tired as everyone else. Standing side by side, they watched silently as the first semi and the parade of cops left the yard.

"I am so glad that all that money
is finally leaving my county. I haven't
slept a wink since we discovered it."

Buck just nodded. They watched in
silence as the last State police car in
the first convoy left the yard.

"Gonna be pretty quiet around here
after all of this", said Buck.

"That's OK, Buck. I think we have
all had as much excitement as we can
stand.   It will be nice to get back to
just regular old boring police work."

Buck smiled and the Sheriff looked
at him. "You are a hell of a cop, Buck
Taylor, and if you ever want to settle
down in one place I can find a spot for
you right here. It would be an honor to
have you in my department."

Buck looked back at her. "It would
be an honor for me to work here. You
guys are top notch. Speaking of top
notch where is Terry Rubin?"

"I told Terry to leave after the
press conference and get some sleep. He
was dead on his feet. You know, Buck,
Terry may be too shy to say something but
you letting him run this investigation
and sticking by him meant a lot to him.
Another big fan in the Buck Taylor fan
club. Ok. I'm heading home to see my
husband and get some sleep. Thanks Buck.
You need anything just call. Stop and
say goodbye on your way out of town."

Buck shook the Sheriff's hand and she headed for her car. She looked back and said. "Oh, stop by your temporary office. I left all your gear in there. Later Buck."

Buck gave a small salute and headed towards his car.

The events of the past couple days hadn't completely sunk in yet and Buck found it hard to believe that this all happened in less than a week. What had happened in this small mountain town this week was incredible and Buck felt privileged to have been able to work with such amazing professionals. Not a bad word could be said about anyone involved in this investigation. Buck felt very proud. He also wished that he could call Lucy and let her know everything had turned out OK. He realized that she probably already knew. The thought made him smile.

On the way back to the Sheriff's office, Buck called each of his kids. By now the story was big news on every TV and radio station in the country, possibly the world, and Buck wanted to make sure they knew he was OK. They were all amazed at the news reports and all expressed how proud they were of their dad.

Chapter Fifty Nine

Buck spent most of the next two days wrapping up loose ends and filing his reports for both this investigation and the triple homicide in Teller County. Buck was a stickler for details and his reports always reflected that. Earlier this afternoon, he had spent a couple hours fly fishing in the Animas River just north of town. He loved living in Colorado and never wanted to be anyplace else.

The La Bon Café was fairly empty when Buck walked in. He was heading back to Gunnison tonight and he wanted one more of Jimmy Palumbo's monster cheeseburgers. He also wanted to fill Jimmy in on the investigation. Loraine had gotten back home the day before and they both stood there listening to Buck tell his tale. They were fascinated. Occasionally one of them would walk away to take care of a customer, but for the most part they just stood behind the bar and listened.

Buck was just finishing up his burger and fries, when the door to the bar opened. Sandi Calhoun stood in the doorway for a moment and removed her sunglasses so her eyes could adjust to the "ambiance." She walked over to Loraine at the cash register and said,

"I was told I might find Buck Taylor here?"

Loraine looked her up and down. Sandi was wearing black jeans, black running shoes, a white button-down blouse open at the neck and a little silver cross around her neck. She had on a black Colorado Rockies ball cap. Loraine must have approved of what she saw because she pointed towards the end of the bar. Sandi spotted Buck sitting on the last bar stool.

Buck looked up as Sandi approached. He said, "Evening Counselor. Surprised to see you here."

Sandi looked around the room. "What a great place. I can understand why you come here. Chief Chandler told me I might find you here. Hope you don't mind?"

Buck smiled. "Not at all. Can I get you something?"

She looked at the back bar. "Do you think they have Dr. Pepper here?"

Buck laughed. "Boy are you in the right place. If Jimmy stopped drinking

Dr. Pepper, the company's stock would drop like a rock. Hey Jimmy. One Jimmy's private reserve for my guest please."

Jimmy walked over and set a glass and a cold can of Dr Pepper on the bar. Buck introduced him to Sandi and they chitchatted for a minute. Buck suggested they move to a table along the wall and he led her to the last table. Buck sat with his back to the wall facing the door. Force of habit.

Sandi said. "I wanted to thank you again for the call. Those kids would have just gotten lost in the system if it hadn't been for you"

Buck asked how they were doing and Sandi filled him in on the last couple days. All the kids had been transported back to Denver and were currently undergoing detox. The last two kids were still in the hospital. The one that had been airlifted to Denver was now in stable condition and the one here in Durango was being released today. That's why Sandi was still in town. She wanted to make sure the kid was taken care of. She had a charter flight later this evening and would be taking the kid with her. Buck was pleased to hear that things were going well. He felt bad for those kids. None of them had asked for this and they certainly didn't deserve what happened to them. They were going to need long term care and a lot of support to get past this nightmare.

Buck's phone was sitting on the table and his text notification alarm chimed. He looked down at the phone, saw a message from Hank Clancy, FBI. He clicked on the text and smiled. The message read simply. "WE GOT HIM."

"Something good?" Sandi asked.

"Let's just say that the kids who decide to return home will find the danger considerably less than it was earlier today."

Sandi looked at him. He turned his phone around and slid it over to her. She looked at the message, her mouth opened, and her hand moved up to her mouth.

She looked at Buck. "Does this mean what I think it means?"

Buck nodded. "I believe it does."

She slid the phone back to Buck. "Oh my God. That is great news."

They chatted about the investigation for a few minutes and Buck told her how impressed he was with the way she handled Bob Townsend, the ICE Agent in Charge. They both laughed. Then Sandi got a serious look on her face.

"I understand you lost your wife
recently. I was very sorry to hear that.
How are you doing?"

Buck thanked her for asking and
told her he was doing alright. His kids
made sure of that. He told her that Lucy
had fought metastatic breast cancer for
over five years, but that once it
metastasized to her brain, it was just a
matter of time. Sandi mentioned her own
battle with breast cancer and that she
understood what he had gone through. She
asked if Lucy had passed away at home.
Buck's eyes got a little moist.

"She passed away in her sleep. We
were lying in bed and I was reading a
report. Lucy had been sleeping twenty
hours a day by then. At one point she
snuggled up against my chest and nestled
in. I must have dozed off and when I
woke up about an hour later Lucy was
gone."

Sandi had tears in her eyes. "I am
so sorry Buck. I shouldn't have brought
that up. What a beautiful way to go.
She was very lucky to have you."

Buck just nodded. It took him a
minute to compose himself. "Yeah. We
were lucky to have each other."

They talked for a few more minutes
then Sandi looked at her watch. She had
a plane to catch and Buck needed to hit
the road. They stood up and Sandi came
around the table and gave Buck a big hug.

"You are a good man Buck and God has blessed you."

Buck smiled and thanked her. He wasn't so sure that was true but coming from her he almost believed it. Sandi waved goodbye to Jimmy and Loraine and left the bar. Buck sat back down and finished his drink. It would be nice to get home. He hadn't been there much lately. He was ready for a little down time. He had a lot of chores to take care of and there were still a lot of memories of Lucy in the house that he hadn't dealt with yet. It was time.

His phone rang and Buck looked at the number. He answered his phone.

"Yes Sir."

The Director asked him if he seen the news yet tonight. Buck said he hadn't. It appears that the investigation had discovered how the trucks got across the border. The FBI was reporting that four Border Crossing Agents assigned to the area around Aqua Prieta in Arizona, had been working for the cartel. The FBI was calling it a huge break in the Durango investigation and the arrests would close a huge hole in our border security.

Buck was pleased. He thanked the Director and hung up. Well that was one question answered. He wondered if they would ever find the answers to the other questions.

Buck walked over and said goodbye
to Jimmy and Loraine and they promised to
get together soon. Buck headed home.

322

Epilogue

In a windowless bunker, somewhere in a secure location in the mountains of central Georgia, two US Air Force drone pilots sat at their control panels and looked at the video feed from the two Predator drones that were now flying high over the desert in Mexico about 40 miles south of the New Mexico border. Below the first drone was a huge hacienda. Over the last several hours, the pilot using his Hi Def camera had been watching as several dozen cars had arrived. The occupants of the cars had entered the hacienda and were greeted by a dark-haired man wearing a white suit. Each car also contained several men, all armed with assault rifles, who remained outside the hacienda. If the pilot so desired, he could have zoomed in enough with the camera to read the serial numbers on the guns.

The other drone was on station about five miles west of the hacienda and was observing a long one-story block building. It appeared to be a warehouse

of some kind. At this moment there was
no movement outside the building. The
pilot waited patiently.

In another windowless room, deep
inside the Pentagon, a dozen high ranking
civilian and military officials were
watching two huge Hi Def monitors mounted
to the wall. They were seeing the same
thing the drone pilots in Georgia were
seeing.

A technician, seated at a computer
console, looked up from his monitor.

"General. Target is confirmed.
The man in the white suit is Carlos
Rojas."

The General looked across the table
at the United States Attorney General.

The Attorney General looked around
the room and each person nodded in
agreement.

"Give the order General", he said.

The general pushed the talk button
on the console in front of him.

"Stingray One One, this is Ranger.
Target is confirmed. You are clear to
execute under my authority."

In the secure bunker in Georgia,
the first drone pilot responded.
"Roger." He lifted a bright red cover on
his console and flipped a switch.
"Weapon is armed. Target is locked." He

pushed the red button next to the cover. "Weapon released."

Back in the basement room in the Pentagon, everyone was silent as they watched the video. Thirty thousand feet above the hacienda, the latching pins released and a massive bomb began to fall. The United States had just declared war on the Sonoma Cartel. Technically, we had also just secretly attacked a foreign country, but all those denials would come later.

The weapon that had been dropped was a fuel air bomb, typically identified as MOAB, mother of all bombs. This was a smaller version of MOAB, but was still unbelievably powerful. According to military sources, the MOAB was the most powerful, non-nuclear explosive device in our arsenal. Several years ago, the Russians had tested their own device dubbed FOAB, father of all bombs. The explosion that resulted was the most powerful explosion ever recorded. It was rumored that they had developed an even more powerful bomb but that they were afraid to test it for fear it might set the atmosphere on fire.

The device technically explodes twice. Five hundred feet above the target the first explosion released billions of atomized, highly explosive fuel particles into the atmosphere, a nanosecond behind this release a second explosion ignited the particles, unleashing a massive fireball on the target. Everything within two hundred yards of ground zero was immediately incinerated. Anything that might have survived the initial fireball was immediately destroyed by the shock wave that emanated from the center of the explosion. Nothing would survive in an area a half mile surrounding ground zero.

Back in the desert, Carlos Rojas had no idea he had only seconds to live, along with many of his hand selected inner circle. He thought nothing could ever touch him. He thought he was protected. He was sadly mistaken and because of his arrogance, his family would pay a heavy price.

Even from thirty thousand feet, the explosion was massive and everyone in the Pentagon room had to turn away as the flash filled the screen. When the Mexican authorities finally arrived on the scene later that day, all they would find was a smoldering crater in the ground two hundred yards wide and almost twenty feet deep. They would be unable to explain what had happened.

At that very moment in the National Earthquake Information Center in Golden, Colorado, several seismographs would register a five point two magnitude earthquake. The epicenter of the quake was located in the Mexican desert approximately forty miles south of the New Mexico border.

As the bomb was being dropped on the hacienda, the second drone's camera was focused on eight figures that seemed to suddenly rise up out of the desert like some kind of hairy plant. Only these hairy plants were armed with the latest high-tech assault rifles. The Pentagon group watched as those eight figures raced toward the block building. A small explosion happened at the entry door and six of the eight figures entered the building while two remained outside. Unlike the video feed from the hacienda, this one had both video and audio.

Everyone in the Pentagon room was mesmerized. It felt like they were watching a video game, only this one involved real bullets, which were now systematically taking out other bad actors with assault rifles and pistols. The automatic weapons fire stopped, and a voice confirmed the all clear. The video showed padlocks being cut and someone yelling for everyone to get out.

The drone video confirmed the action as the front door swung open and dozens of people ran from the building and scattered into the desert. The six Special Operations team members ran out and joined up with their two team mates outside. The entire operation had taken less than two minutes to complete.

A voice came over the loud speaker. "Ranger, this is Striker One. Building is clear. Mission accomplished."

The General keyed his mike. "Roger, Striker One. Confirmation received."

The video showed the men running across the desert and jumping into a waiting Blackhawk helicopter. The video ended and was replaced with the video feed from the drone.

"Stingray One Two, this is Ranger. Target confirmed. Execute on my authority."

Inside the bunker in Georgia, the second drone pilot acknowledged the order and followed the same procedure as the first pilot. As he pushed the red button, two hellfire missiles headed on an unstoppable course toward the block building. Two massive explosions occurred almost simultaneously. The block building was destroyed.

Without any further communication, the two drone pilots headed their drones back to a secret drone base operating out of the White Sands Testing Center in New Mexico. Once the drones were secure, the pilots shut down their console and left the structure.

In the room deep in the Pentagon, the Attorney General congratulated the General on a successful mission. They had just sent a strong message to the other active cartels that the United States would not sit idly by if they chose to move their business north of the

border. The General then nodded to the
technician seated at the computer
console. The technician pushed the
delete button on the keyboard and all
evidence of the attacks disappeared.
The President nodded and left the room.

ACKNOWLEGEMENTS

A special thank you to my daughter Christina J Morgan, my unofficial editor-in-chief. She devoted a significant amount of time making sure the book was presented as perfectly as possible. Any mistakes the reader may find are solely the responsibility of the author.

Also, I would like to thank my family for all their encouragement. I have been telling them stories since they were little and I always told them that someone should be writing this stuff down. I finally decided to write it down myself.

I want to thank my closest friend, Trish Moakler Herud. She has been encouraging me for years to write my stories down. I hope this will make her proud.

Finally, a very special thanks to my late wife Jane. She had pushed me for years to become a writer and my biggest regret is that she didn't live long enough to see it happen. I love her with all my heart and miss her every day. I think she would be pleased.

ABOUT THE AUTHOR

Chuck Morgan has been a Construction Project Manager for over thirty years. He is an avid fly fisherman and outdoorsmen and loves hiking, camping and mountain biking. His first book was published in early 2017. It was a nonfiction account of his late wife's nine-year battle with metastatic breast cancer. It was titled HER NAME WAS JANE by Charles E Morgan. Chuck thinks of himself as more than just an author. He is a story teller. His writing philosophy is simple. Develop the characters, drop them into a situation, step aside and let the characters lead the way. This book is the start of a series of novels involving his lead character Buck Taylor.

Follow Buck Taylor's latest
investigation in

CRIME DELAYED

Coming in early 2018